# Tales from Havasu
## Vol XI

COLLECTED WORKS

OF THE

LAKE HAVASU WRITERS GROUP

2022

## OASIS COMMITTEE

Production: Tim Montbriand, Karen VanderJagt

Beverly Jackson, Jane Schopen

Publishing: Jim Veary, EV Medina

Cover Art: Anne Vandegrift

Copyright© 2022
All rights reserved. The copyright for each story
is held by the individual author

No portion of this book may be reproduced in whole or part,
or stored in a retrieval system or transmitted in any form
or by any means without the permission of the individual author.

ISBN: 9798788469942
**2nd Edition**

Printed in the United States of America

# DEDICATION

Over the years, from our founding members to the present, the Lake Havasu Writers' Group has taken the love of a good story and has tried to bring out the best in each other to tell that story. We have written and read many submissions, giving our honest praise and helpful criticisms. We may never make the New York Times Best Seller List, or win a Pulitzer Prize, but we can say we pursued our passion, and that makes us writers.

We also want to say a special thank you to our families who put up with our many quirks, especially when we say, "Listen to this."

# PREFACE

The Lake Havasu City Writers Group (LHCWG) publishes this bi-annual anthology, previously titled *The Oasis,* but now called *Tales from Havasu.* The stories herein are of two types: The long stories address topics of the writer's choice and can be of any genre, but they have a suggested word limit of one thousand words. The LHCWG has learned over time that word limits enhance members' self-editing skills, making for clear, concise writing.

The short stories, with a suggested word limit of 250 words and choice of any genre, have been written in response to a prompt, which is provided for the reader. As you read, think about what you might have written in response to the prompt. You'll be amazed at the number of possibilities.

The LHCWG has also adopted the following convention: Italics, in addition to designating long works—novels, plays, movies, etc.—is used herein to indicate a character's thoughts or a word that is emphasized in dialogue.

We members of the LHCWG hope that you enjoy these stories and share them with family and friends. But, just as importantly, we hope that you are inspired to write and find a pleasurable, creative, emotional, and intellectual outlet for a lifetime.

# TABLE OF CONTENTS

| Title | Author | Page |
|---|---|---|
| **Sky King** | Jim Veary | 1 |
| **The Visit** | T.A. Novak | 2 |
| **Having it All** | Mary Corrao | 3 |
| **A Franklin Bullseye** | Larry Quackenboss | 4 |
| **The Change** | Jane Schopen | 5 |
| **Believe it or Not** | Karen VanderJagt | 6 |
| **Escaping Death** | Tim Montbriand | 7 |
| **Bad Luck Saloon** | Beverly Jackson | 10 |
| **Blood Sucker** | Beverly Jackson | 11 |
| **Closing Its Doors** | Karen VanderJagt | 12 |
| **Duncan's Last Hurrah** | Beverly Jackson | 14 |
| **Christmas Mem** | Jane Schopen | 15 |
| **A Hallmark Christmas** | Jim Veary | 16 |
| **The Soul Seeker** | Beverly Jackson | 32 |
| **Skeletal Rage** | Jane Schopen | 33 |
| **Delayed Revenge** | Claudia Haeckel | 35 |
| **The Chat** | Jim Veary | 42 |
| **Do Not Mourn Me** | Pat Leso | 45 |
| **Crow's Funeral** | Claudia Haeckel | 46 |
| **Death Be Not Prod** | Tim Montbriand | 48 |
| **Duffy Dawg's Ball** | Claudia Haeckel | 51 |
| **Warrior's Lament** | Karen VanderJagt | 52 |
| **Dropouts and Losers** | Jane Schopen | 53 |
| **Go Greyhound** | Tim Montbriand | 54 |
| **The Elephant in the Park** | Beverly Jackson | 57 |
| **Searching for Gargantua** | Jim Veary | 58 |
| **Dust to Dust** | Jane Schopen | 61 |

| Title | Author | Page |
|---|---|---|
| **No One Gets Out Alive** | Pat Leso | 62 |
| **Mars or Bust** | Pat Leso | 63 |
| **For their Own Good** | Jane Schopen | 78 |
| **The Hitchhiker** | Karen VanderJagt | 79 |
| **From a Booster** | Jane Schopen | 80 |
| **The Funniest Man Alive** | Mary Corrao | 81 |
| **Crossing the Highway** | Claudia Haeckel | 82 |
| **Got Karma?** | Tim Montbriand | 86 |
| **Johnny Angel** | Pat Leso | 90 |
| **Last Visit to Sids** | T.A. Novak | 91 |
| **Whenever I Want You** | Karen VanderJagt | 92 |
| **The Hand of Gramma Cupie** | Jane Schopen | 93 |
| **If Mamma Don't Sleep** | Jane Schopen | 95 |
| **Green Acres** | Tim Montbriand | 96 |
| **Albina** | Mary Corrao | 99 |
| **An Escape to Freedom** | T.A. Novak | 102 |
| **A Killer Smile** | Mary Corrao | 107 |
| **Bytes Dog Man** | Tim Montbriand | 108 |
| **The One that Got a Weigh** | Jim Veary | 109 |
| **Guilty Plea? Sure!** | Tim Montbriand | 110 |
| **A Simple Solution** | Beverly Jackson | 112 |
| **Justice is in the Bite** | Beverly Jackson | 113 |
| **And Then There was One** | Pat Leso | 114 |
| **His Final Epitaph** | Karen VanderJagt | 116 |
| **High and Dry** | Tim Montbriand | 120 |
| **Imagination Destination** | T.A. Novak | 123 |
| **The Last Straw** | Mary Corrao | 124 |
| **Wild Turkey, Double Shot** | Jane Schopen | 125 |
| **Heaven's Rainbow** | Larry Quackenboss | 126 |

| Title | Author | Page |
|---|---|---|
| **I'm Hooked** | T.A. Novak | 127 |
| **Running on Empty** | Tim Montbriand | 130 |
| **Killing Time** | Mary Corrao | 133 |
| **Magic Hands** | Mary Corrao | 134 |
| **Let The Rumpus Begin** | Jane Schopen | 135 |
| **The Letter** | Larry Quackenboss | 136 |
| **The Little Red Schoolhouse** | Larry Quackenboss | 137 |
| **Revenge...** | Tim Montbriand | 138 |
| **Yard Work** | Jim Veary | 141 |
| **The Long Drive Home** | Claudia Haeckel | 145 |
| **Lying Nights** | Larry Quackenboss | 146 |
| **The Match** | Tim Montbriand | 147 |
| **One Can Only Try** | Karen VanderJagt | 153 |
| **Moon Dance** | Jim Veary | 154 |
| **Moonlight Kisses** | T.A. Novak | 155 |
| **Not The Olden Days** | Mary Corrao | 157 |
| **Politics** | Karen VanderJagt | 159 |
| **Portrait** | Karen VanderJagt | 160 |
| **Share the Road Rage** | Tim Montbriand | 162 |
| **The Avenging Angel** | Larry Quackenboss | 165 |
| **Things Gone with the Wind** | Tim Montbriand | 170 |
| **Time to Move On** | Mary Corrao | 171 |
| **Taking the Bait** | Jane Schopen | 172 |
| **Prick of the Needle** | Karen VanderJagt | 173 |
| **Space Junket** | Tim Montbriand | 175 |
| **Stand your Ground** | Mary Corrao | 177 |
| **Call a Marine** | Jim Veary | 178 |
| **Adrift** | T.A. Novak | 188 |
| **Stars and Beyond** | Larry Quackenboss | 192 |
| **Happy Birthday** | Daniel Fraga | 194 |

# Lake Havasu City High School Writing Competition Winners

| Award | Author | Title | Page |
|---|---|---|---|
| First Place | Kayla Maserang | The Stain | 199 |
| Second Place | Luci Towner | Seeds in the Wind | 202 |
| Third Place | Damari Campos | Morning Glory | 205 |

# Tales from Havasu
## Vol XI

Flash prompt: Bucket List

## Sky King
by Jim Veary

My earliest childhood memories go back to 1951 and the image of a five-year-old me sitting on the living room floor in front of a huge floor model console radio. The big illuminated dial was a half circle of magical promises. With the twist of a knob, I could bring the whole world into the room to entertain me. There was "Abbot & Costello," "Flash Gordon," and, when my parents would let me stay up a bit later, "Inner Sanctum." But my all-time favorite, the show I never missed, was "Sky King" Its lead character was an Arizona rancher and pilot. King, and his niece, Penny, lived on the Flying Crown Ranch, catching criminals and spies using his airplane, the *Songbird*.

My favorite part of the show was the sound effects at the very beginning. I would sit in front of that radio and listen to King's Cessna roar down the runway toward me, the twin engines racing as it approached. At the very last moment, before it could run me over, the airplane lifted off and thundered over my head. What a thrill!

I didn't have a clue what a bucket list was, but somewhere in the middle of my fifth year of life, I suddenly decided upon the first and most important item on my bucket list. I wanted to be a pilot. I wanted to soar off the ground with the sound of thunder and grab a piece of sky.

It took me another forty-six years to make that happen.

Flash prompt: Bucket List

# The Visit
## by T.A. Novak

I could barely see his eyes—if they were eyes. The hood drooped low covering what I thought was a face. A plume of musty-smelling dust expelled into the space between us as he said "You're going to die." It was a quivering, raspy voice, sounding as if it were emanating from a dank dark grave.

"Tell me something I don't know."

Dust billowed from under the hood with the words that followed: "You dare joust with me?"

I could see his bony hand clench the scythe he held while the other pointed at my chest, emphasizing each question. "Have you fulfilled your life's dreams? Your ambitions? Completed your list?"

The moon emerged from behind a cloud, and I could see my midnight visitor more clearly. His long, moth-eaten cloak hung over his shoulders, its sleeves nearly covering the hand pointing at me.

"What list? I've done most things I've wanted to do in my life." I paused. "Within my means, of course. If you have a few thousand to spare, I could dream up a couple more."

"You're not taking me seriously, are you?"

"You ever look in a mirror? You're a bad dream, nothing more."

Sparks and smoke filled the air as my visitor shouted, "Most would beg for more time."

I got out of bed, popped three Tums and emptied my bladder. I had eaten too late and needed to pee.

Thirty minutes later, Gina Lollobrigida and I were tussling between the sheets.

Some dreams are very good, some not so much.

Flash prompt: Bucket List

# Having It All
## by Mary Corrao

DON'T OPEN UNLESS I'M DEAD.

I discovered the note on the bag in my closet the morning after he left.

Ronnie, The Mouth, Saparelli, irresistible and dangerous, swaggered into my detective agency three weeks ago. He was good looking in an Italian way with intense bedroom eyes and dark hair that curled at the back of his neck.

Why he wanted to hire me was vague. But when I felt his breath on my skin as he leaned in toward me, I didn't care.

He proposed that we discuss business over a drink. The drink turned to dinner; dinner turned to breakfast. I'm not in the habit of spending the night with clients, but most of my sparse list of clients were not close to beddable.

Three days later, in the morning paper, I read about his untimely demise. As desirable as Ronnie was, my income barely covered my expenses. Therefore, the news of his death left me with mixed feelings, kind of like hearing your great aunt died while you were having an orgasm.

I waited for news about missing money and even placed an anonymous call to the police. Nothing.

I sat on my bed, emptied the bag, and luxuriated in the sea of green bills. Plans for my bucket list began sprouting like spring dandelions. That's when I noticed the note at the bottom of the bag.

*\*\*\**

I'm sipping my drink in a lovely island paradise. Ronnie leans in, planting his lips on mine. They don't call him Ronnie the Mouth for nothing. How could that be you ask? It's all about having it all.

# A Franklin Bullseye

by Larry Quackenboss

The whole bar watched as Angie leaned over the pool table. It wasn't the shot she was making but the shot she was giving. Her muscled butt stretched the mini skirt to the point of breaking, and her cowgirl boots added three more inches to long and lean, thirty-three-inch legs. Four buttons down and a hint of black against the pale white skin gave every man a lusty thought or two. She moved around the table with the grace of a dancer and a look of unrestrained sexuality.

"Eight ball side pocket," she said. Letting the cue move back and forth in her hand with a sexual meaning, she lined up the shot.

Every man leaned forward, hoping to hide the events happening in his jeans. A couple downed their shots, and LeRoy just took his battered and stained cowboy hat off and began fanning his belt buckle. "Damn, that girl sure can start a man on fire," he said to no one in particular, placing the hat back on his head.

Angie stroked the stick with a caress that the boys could only wish she would do to them. She lined up the shot and hit the cue ball dead center. It rolled across the table and softly touched the eight ball rolling to the edge of the pocket only to have it slip on by.

The cue dropped on the felt as she reached into her pocket.

"Here's your fifty dollars, LeRoy," she said, tossing the bill on the table. "How about I get a do-over for a Franklin?" she asked.

"Okay, same shot, same way," LeRoy said.

Flash Prompt: Hot as Hell

# The Change

by Jane Schopen

Genny woke at two in the morning and feared she must be ill. Her skin prickled with sweat as a heat wave engulfed her. The room felt stifling! She bolted out of bed away from the summer quilt and away from the sleeping husband who radiated like a blast furnace.

Even in darkness, she deftly navigated narrow hallways, stairs, and cluttered rooms to the back porch. She'd walked this path countless times during her forty-eight years on the family farm: following sisters, sneaking out to meet a sweetie, and chasing her own kids.

Outside, the dank Iowa air gave no relief until she wandered over to the vegetable garden. There, a shy breeze stirred and lifted the nightgown from her sticky flesh. She sighed as the fever passed. *Oh, I'm not sick.*

A yellow dog loped over from her post by the barn. In the moonlight, old Lizzie's body sagged and swayed as she moved. The retriever always brought a gift—this time it was a chewed-up corn cob that Genny acted pleased to receive.

"Thanks, my friend," she murmured to the dog. "You and I have birthed a lot of pups, haven't we? Think I'm going through the change, so that's it for me now."

Lizzie looked sympathetic, then yawned large.

Genny laughed and said, "I know, it's part of life. To everything there is a season and all of that lofty stuff."

Now chilled, she hugged the corncob against her chest and rocked from side to side. How she loved the earthy smells of fertile soil and sweet, dewy plants.

Flash prompt: Magical Mystery Tour

## Believe It or Not

by Karen VanderJagt

"Welcome to our 'Mythology' zoo where we bring the magical past to life." Tomas led the group to the enclosures. "Please follow all my instructions."

At the first enclosure, everyone saw a snow-white unicorn through the glass. "Are any of you ill?" Tomas asked.

One man stepped forward. "I have emphysema."

Tomas took the man's hand and placed it in a small opening. The unicorn touched its horn to his hand and everyone saw a spark.

"You are cured," Tomas said as the man took a deep breath.

The next enclosure revealed an emerald dragon. "Any quandaries?" Tomas asked pointing to a speaker.

"I do," said a young woman. "Do I marry Davey or Tommy?"

The dragon rumbled, "Neither is right. Continue your studies."

"Thank you."

The third area held a small pool inhabited by a raven-haired mermaid. A man asked "What does she do?"

"I'm afraid I can't let you have any contact. Her song drives men insane." The mermaid winked.

"We come to our last viewing, and I won't raise the shade. Look at the monitor only because to look into the Gorgon's eyes will turn you to stone."

A middle-aged man scoffed. "Really? You expect us to believe all this? Can you prove any of this? It's all show." As the others looked at the monitor, he flipped up the shade. No one heard a sound.

Sighing, Tomas pulled down the shade, looked at the statue and said, "Put him in the garden with the others."

# Escaping Death
## by Tim Montbriand

He opened his eyes to a dim room illuminated intermittently with green light, a woman moving furtively about the foot of his bed. Oh God, what was she doing? He had a metallic taste in his mouth that seemed linked by a metallic thread to a burning stitch in his side. He was scared by his inability to understand the room, the woman, his pain. He blacked out.

His reality became a series of waking moments, synesthetic dreams of palpably smooth spaces confused with the actual room in which he lay. Often when he opened his eyes he sensed a woman at the foot of his bed intent upon him, making him feel naked and vulnerable. She looked familiar, but he didn't know why, his inability to makes sense of her presence adding to his confusion. The furtive lady, inexplicably, seemed to be hanging laundry off in his peripheral vision. He had lost his sense of existing solidly in time, floating back and forth from a surrealistic dreamland to a hard-edged world that kept trying to assert itself as reality.

He slept and woke again, the room now registering upon him as small and distant. He saw his wife, looking much older than she should, her helmet of brown hair now graying, her body stooped. He spoke to her, "What's going on, Helen?" She started at the sound of his voice, a pitying look on her face. She started to rise until the woman always hanging laundry and lurking about on rubber-soled shoes held her back. Before he lost consciousness again—shifted worlds—he resolved to check the emaciated rib cage his arm had rubbed against to see if it really were his own.

He wasn't quite sure when he first recognized that he was in a hospital room or nursing home, or when his wife stopped visiting him. Every time he had spoken to his wife, she cried, her facial features contorting in dismay. But she never spoke to him. The ubiquitous nurse spoke to him but never responded either. "What's wrong with me?" he would ask her. "We'll make you comfortable," the nurse would reply as she wiped around his mouth, a tender gesture that saddened him somehow. The woman's behavior seemed capricious to him, shifting between callousness and solicitude.

His acute sense of pain gradually receded to a dulling physical malaise. He seemed constantly to feel exposed to a chilling draft by the too-small cotton gown he wore tied at his neck. He was penned in by the rails of the bed hung with plastic receptacles like milk jugs. A television set mounted to the wall droned on relentlessly, its seriousness and urgency frightening and disturbing him somehow. Near his head was a beeping monitor, a telemetric god sending information to an apathetic, receptor. Tubes and bags surrounded him, engulfed him, seemed to emanate from him.

Always on his first awakening within the curtained chrysalis of privacy, he became aware of shadowy, soft-footed figures flitting across the doorway and was assaulted by the smell of decay a dentist's drill produces. The one comfort in the room was the window through which he experienced a flight of mind beyond the enclosing walls as did Wordsworth's nun in her narrow convent or the schoolboy in his lonely citadel.

Nameless emotions, those nuanced, indefinable feelings often inseparable from thought came to him without sequence or dates. Light from the window evoked memories of different days: In bright summer, he felt the hum of timeless days, the incessant cicada heralding eternity. Sometimes snow would fall on the window sill, and he remembered how big snowfalls suspended the pressures of everyday obligations and brought together neighbors helping each other dig out and reach for no other destination than freedom. A large tree outside showed bright red pointed leaves, and he felt the bite of fall days, stringent and cool, so unlike the moist, cloying sweetness of his room. He sensed the springtime, too--maybe even more than the other seasonal shifts—in the warmth and the breeze and the birdsong. Although it was more a feeling than a coherent thought, the seasons seemed to be moving too fast like the images on a slot machine—random and incongruous.

One day, the furtive woman wheeled him to an open window and said something about "an airing." He wanted desperately to be in the outside freshness and out of the staleness inside the time clog that was this room. It seemed simple enough to move out into that space even though he didn't even know what floor he was on, it didn't matter.

He put his right arm out over the sill and tried to pull himself out, but he hadn't the strength. He lay back a moment to rest, feeling, however, a palpable urgency. Once he had regained some strength, he raised himself up feebly onto his elbows and with a rocking motion eventually rolled onto the sill chest first. He inch-wormed his way to the edge and moved the center of his weight far enough that he fell to the ground.

He heard something snap but felt no pain as he landed and rolled on the ground to the edge of a meadow The smell of the grass was a strong sedative and a siren call back to his innocent youth as was the sight of the small pond ringed with tall grass and small saplings. He felt more and more a feeling of contentment as he emerged from what seemed like longer and longer naps. He knew he was dying and entertained his last thought, if what he knew in his very being could be called a "thought": Now that he had broken the deadlock space of physical confinement, maybe he could move through time to unending moments of peace and comfort.

An orderly sent to retrieve the now available hospital bed said aloud to the empty room, "Why are the wheels jacked up higher on one side of the bed?"

Flash prompt: Golden Horseshoe Saloon

## Bad Luck Saloon
### by Beverly Jackson

"See that square section between those two tall skyscrapers? No? Come closer. Yeah, that's right. Look between the rails of those wrought iron gates."

I peered through the black vertical spires with a black horseshoe hanging upside down adorning the center, and then looked wide-eyed at Uncle Jimmy. "It's a cemetery!"

"Yup, that's what it is alright but wasn't always so. Skyscrapers weren't there either. Why, we're talking a few centuries ago. Used to be the famous Golden Horseshoe Saloon and Brothel, owned and operated by your great grandpa, Joseph Powell. He be buried somewhere in this here cemetery, not sure where on account of he didn't have no proper burial."

"How come?"

"Well, your grandpa was a mean-spirited old coot. He screwed a lotta good folks along the way, one woman in particular."

"Really? Tell me. What happened?"

"Her name was Simply Sue, and she owned and ran the brothel above the saloon. One night, Miss Sue caught your grandpa stealing earnings what was meant for her girls. She pointed a rifle at his head and told him he had two choices—either put the money back or die. Joseph came at her full of rage screaming, 'Like hell I will,' and Sue shot him right between the eyes. He fell backwards, knocking a kerosene lantern over. Flames engulfed the whole building in minutes, and everyone inside perished.

They never rebuilt that Bad Luck Saloon, just made it a cemetery, on account of so many people dying, and encircled it with this here wrought iron fence and hung that horseshoe turned upside down."

Flash Prompt: Dracula's Retirement Plan

## Blood Sucker

by Beverly Jackson

Here I sit in the courtroom alone. Everyone has left including my now ex-wife and her lawyer, who I could see was already smitten by her beauty.

Dazed, I ponder my past. I was a day trader on Wall Street when I met Draga, a Romanian beauty. She was an au pair for the children of my best friend, Sam, and his wife, Sheila. I met her when I was invited to their home for dinner.

Cupid's arrow hit its mark the moment I saw her. She had long jet-black hair with blue-green eyes and a figure that wouldn't quit. Now that I look back, I realize that she didn't seem that interested in me until Sam mentioned that I was brilliant at what I did and that I would, one day, run the company I worked for. That was the beginning of the end.

It was a whirlwind romance followed by a quickie marriage at the court house. We were in love...or at least I was. Our first ten years together were pretty good. Then I got promoted to vice president of my firm with a substantial increase in pay. That's when my marriage, and my life, began to crumble.

Draga, whom I now refer to as "Dracula," sued me for divorce and now gets our home, half my income, *and* half my future income. I am drained but no longer blind. I see it clearly now. This was *her* retirement plan.

Flash prompt: One Last Bash in the Retirement Home

## Closing Its Doors
by Karen VanderJagt

"Where are you going to go?" asked eighty-five-year-old Gladys.

"I don't know," replied ninety-year-old Edgar. "My family can't be bothered."

"I can't believe the retirement home is closing after all these years," Betty sobbed.

"There's no money. Government won't pay squat, and folks don't want to work for what they get paid here," Edgar sneered.

"We gotta do something," Gladys said, thinking about the situation. "We can make the money, can't we?"

Tony joined them, looking as distinguished as always with his silver-tipped cane. "I have friends who might help." Mysterious Tony had all sorts of friends.

So the group, helped by Tony's friends, came up with a plan to solve the financial problems of their home. They worked hard over the next two weeks memorizing their lines and practicing their parts until they were ready. This was going to be a show everyone would remember. They'd go down in the books.

They made reservations for the van to take them on a trip downtown that coming Friday.

When the day came, Gladys got her hair done in a beautiful silver and dressed in her best royal blue dress with silver accessories. She thought she'd look stunning in the pictures.

Betty had to borrow one of Gladys' dresses and also let her friend fix her hair. Gladys had style.

Edgar put on his last blue suit. It might be old just like he was, but it was considered very stylish in its heyday. He put one of his accessories, a red carnation, in his jacket lapel and another accessory under the seat of his walker next to his oxygen tank.

Tony dressed as he always did. He didn't go out unless he looked dashing. He'd been photographed so often in his life he knew what looked good. Just because hard times had hit, it didn't mean one shouldn't look good.

They took the home's van downtown then walked toward the building. People turned to look at the procession of three smiling, waving elderly people followed by another pushing his walker along as quickly as he could and huffing rather loudly despite the oxygen. They smiled back in return.

At 5:59 PM the troupe entered the bank.

"This is a stick-up," Gladys shouted her opening line.

At first, the guard laughed until Edgar opened the walker seat and handed Tony a gun. The guard then stuffed money into the bag Betty held, and the group smiled their thanks. Tony touched his cane to his forehead in salute as they headed to the door.

The police were outside waiting.

Since they all confessed, the trial was short and sweet. Jail would be their final retirement home. However, the front page story and the photograph of four smiling, well-dressed, elderly people being handcuffed and taken away caused a powerful reaction. A corporate sponsor came forward, so thanks to Depends and the goodwill donations by the public, the doors of Easy Rest Retirement Home would stay open.

Flash Prompt: One Last Bash in the Retirement Home

## Duncan's Last Hoorah
### by Bev Jackson

"Honest, God. It wasn't *all* my fault."

God drummed His fingers on the table. Everything around Duncan rumbled loudly with each tap of God's finger.

Duncan Needlemier shrank from the terrible noise. His body trembled in disbelief. *I can't believe this is my God. I was a faithful servant. One tiny little indiscretion and I'm condemned? What kind of God is this?*

The noise ceased, and God stared at Duncan. "You know, I can hear what you're thinking."

Breath escaped Duncan like air from a punctured balloon. *Oh, shit. Oops.* His eyes grew wide as saucers. "Please, dear God, let me explain."

"Alright," God sighed. "Let's hear it."

"I wanted to bring excitement into the lives of the residents of Sunny Haven, so I made brownies laced with marijuana. I cut a little square of brownie for each person so nobody would eat too much, but I guess if you're old like we are, it doesn't take much. Before I knew it, ninety-year-old Miss Molly was playing with lighted matches, and the retirement home went up in flames. But I sure created a lot of excitement for the old folks."

"Humph." God sighed. "Your intentions were honorable, but your act caused irreparable damage; plus, you died in the fire. Are you sorry?"

"Oh hell yes! I mean, yes Sir."

Suddenly, he was transferred into the most beautiful place he'd ever seen. Duncan Needlemier sighed then smiled. He knew he was in heaven.

Flash Prompt: Ghost of Christmas Past

## Christmas Mem

by Jane Schopen

Fearing dangerous loss of self-control with repeated exposure, Yule engaged memory 1225 only once a year. She herself had unearthed mem1225 while working as a Mem Lab mining engineer. 1225 ranked so high on the evoked response scale that lab monitors buried it under deep encryption—encryption she knew.

Yule recovered and downloaded the mem. She deactivated her protective field and slipped into a virtual suit. Advances in protective equipment and virtual reality technology, along with a highly evolved aversion to socialization, had long ago freed humans from messy body contacts and emotional outpourings. But like other cohorts, Yule snuck small doses of such experiences in the privacy of her own dwelling.

Mems were old, obtained from cryopreserved brains of the twentieth century, a time known for uncontrolled behavior. Historical research had given Yule a better understanding of 1225, titled a "Christmas" remembrance.

Immersion was swift. She huddled under a blanket, whispering with syngenes or "siblings." Yule's skin prickled to life with sensations of warmth and touching bodies. They discussed whether a deity called Santa had come and what he brought.

Biologic breeders known as parents summoned them to an area with incinerating wood and a fragrant, festooned conifer tree. Feelings of intense pleasure overcame Yule at the sight of paper-covered objects. One at a time, the "gifts" were unwrapped, and people cheered. Yule uncovered the replica of a recently incubated child and felt immense satisfaction.

The high point occurred when she handed "mother" a gift. Yule became trapped inside soft arms and perceived…love.

# Hallmark Christmas
by Jim Veary

## Chapter 1

Friends call me Mara, Mara Lago. That's my pen name. Good friends call me Kathy. I don't pen eight-hundred-page novels. I write short-story romances that play out across a hundred pages or less, the kind of things that show up in anthologies or magazines. I'm not nearly as well known as Danielle Steele either. I've never had the staying power to actually create a novel. I'm always too anxious to see how it all ends. So short stories are my forte´. I do have a following. There's my mother, my sister and her book club, and a smattering of unnamed minions.

The past year has mostly dribbled past me like catsup from a narrow-neck bottle.

I've isolated myself in my L.A. apartment, trapped by an unreasonable fear of the Covid pandemic. I churned out a bunch of stories at first, but the market seems to have collapsed for short stories. Eventually I just gave up, and my survival plans focused on pizza, hot dogs, chocolate cake, and Hallmark movies.

Back in the day, my childhood fantasies were all built on a foundation of Hallmark commercials that inevitably left me in happy tears. I couldn't watch those commercials without a full box of tissues nearby. In my youthful naiveté, I imagined my adult life as a series of merging Hallmark commercials, surrounded by loving family and enraptured in situations that always worked out in smiles and tears.

It hasn't worked out quite that way. Oh, I am a cheerful person despite still being unwed, unattached, and also broke. Indeed, I seem to reside at the corner of Indigent Avenue and Pitiable Lane. It would be nice to sell a story or two.

Through my year of Covid isolation, I've become quite the expert on Hallmark films and eventually realized that they are all short stories stretched out to fill a two-hour time slot. Or, in some cases, just one of those old commercials really stretched out to two hours. They all run just about the same, and all leave the viewer in happy tears. I came to the Ah-ha moment when it dawned on me that *I can do that. I can write a screenplay. . . or a teleplay as they call it.* A diligent internet search revealed the existence of a Hallmark Style Sheet that lays out all the rules of making a Hallmark movie. Nothing is left to chance or to the author's individual tastes. Either you do it the Hallmark way, or you shouldn't even bother trying.

So, I'm thinking of a Visa-crunching Christmas trip to Vermont as research for my screenplay—snow, sleigh rides, snowball fights, and après-ski. I'll take copious notes and then try my hand at writing my opus. Hallmark! Get ready to be dazzled.

**The Rules**

The female protagonist—that would be me—must fit into one of a short list of boxes. I actually fill several: a big-city girl, single, and world weary—make that Covid weary.

Next is a narrow selection of career paths. I'm not a baker or a lawyer, but I am a writer. One box is all I need.

The next one is a bit of a stretch as the female protagonist must return to her hometown at Christmas time. Well, Los Angeles *is* my hometown, so a little bending of the truth is required and appropriate. I have a dear friend who owns a beautiful home in Vermont. It would be better if it were a ranch parked at the base of a snow-capped mountain, but a nice house on a snowy street will do as my childhood home.

Then there is my reason for going to Vermont, and, again, I have a problem. All of the suggested motivations are folksy and sentimental. The protagonist must inherit something or save the family business or take part in a festival. That stuff just doesn't happen in real life, only in Hallmark movies, so I have to fake it. For the sake of the plot, I will be going back to Vermont to be the Maid of Honor at my friend's Christmas wedding. I know, it's been done before, but still I've been a

Maid of Honor at a few friends' weddings, so I know how it all works. I can fake it!

Now comes the exciting conclusion and the hardest part of the writing. I have to fall magically in love with one of a few male types: a sensitive guy in tight jeans or an old flame who still carries the torch for me, or a dyed-in-the-wool bachelor and his dog—it helps if the dog turns out to be smarter than the guy—or a widower and his precocious kid. I don't think I can plan that part out. I'll just have to see what is available out there and go with the flow. It's not like I actually plan on falling in love, but a little writer's inspiration would be helpful.

There are a few rules when we get to the timing of the romance. The first attempt at a kiss cannot happen until two-thirds of the script has been used to develop the relationship, and that attempted kiss must be interrupted by a ringing phone or a dog or that precocious child or a black widow spider falling out of the mistletoe.

Then there follows the unfortunate misunderstanding when I see my guy hug another woman, or worse, another man, or worse still, a midget of indeterminate sex. I must leave for the airport in tears to return home while my guy has to chase me down and explain that it was just his sister or his best friend from fifth grade and he loves me, and we fall into one another's arms and kiss as the closing credits roll past, which is just as well cuz no one can get a flight back to L.A. at the last minute on Christmas Eve, not from Rutland, Vermont, anyway.

That's a Hallmark movie in the rough.

\*\*\*

# A Hallmark Christmas

## Chapter 2

The flight to Vermont had one stopover in Chicago. Stop-over is an understatement. I'm not a happy flyer to begin with, and the flight was a raging bull of a roller-coaster as we bounced through a nasty winter storm. I was terrified and found myself clutching my seatmate's arm. He gently removed my hand and clasped it in his own. "You'll be fine," he whispered as he squeezed my hand.

"Are we gonna c-c-crash?" I stuttered.

"Nope. There's no record of a plane ever crashing because of turbulence. We'll be fine." He kept up a spirited conversation and actually did take my mind off the weather right down to a slippery landing when I squeezed all the blood out of the poor guy's hand.

He was right. We landed fine, but the weather had cancelled my connecting flight to Rutland. The airline desk warned that a Nor'easter was rolling into New England and a foot of snow was expected. The speakers in the ceiling crackled, and a voice announced, "The airport will remain closed until late tomorrow afternoon, and all passengers should collect their bags at the carrousel." She added sweetly, "There is a shuttle to the airport hotel available outside the terminal."

I found my bag stuck on the carrousel, a big, ragged hole torn in it with my Disney panties flapping in the breeze. Tucking Mickey and Minnie back into the bag, I set out in search of the hotel shuttle. I found it in a spot marked "Rental cars," but the placard on the front said, "Hotel." It's Chicago. Whatdaya expect?

Ten minutes later, I walked into the hotel to find my hero seatmate in line at the check-in. "We meet again," I greeted him. "I'm Mara, by the way."

"Larry," he replied., "I kinda thought I'd see you here." He looked down to see Minnie winking at him. He smiled. "Mara? That's an unusual name."

"Well," I shuffled my feet. "It's actually my pen name, Mara Lago. I'm a writer. But you can call me Kathy."

"Mara Lago? I don't recall reading anything."

"I just write short stories, magazine pieces, and stuff."

"Ahhh," he replied then turned back to the clerk as she finished his check-in.

I looked him over. He wasn't handsome, but he wasn't hard on the eyes either. Brown hair. I think the eyes were brown. No facial hair. He had a smooth, chiseled face with no deep worry lines. Not too bad at all. But his attraction lay in his smile and his attitude. I immediately liked the guy. When he turned back to me, I could see that his eyes were hazel, and his face wore a frown. "What?" I asked.

"It seems the hotel is full. I got the last room."

"No!"

"Yes."

"There must be . . ."

"Kathy, I stay here often, and I know Jeanette--he gestured to the clerk—and she assured me that this was absolutely the last room available, and that was only because I had a reservation."

"So, what do I do? Is there another hotel?"

"There are many hotels but getting to them would be almost impossible in this weather. You can sleep on one of the lobby couches, and Jeanette could bring you a pillow and blankets or …"

"Or? What or?"

"My room has two queen beds."

"So what? I bunk in with you?"

"Not bunk in," he said with a grin, "You have your own bed. I know how to be a gentleman."

I looked at the clerk. "You know him?"

She smiled and said, "Yes, miss, I do, and he has always been a gentleman."

I stared at the door for a moment and noticed Minnie peeking out of my luggage. *Well, what the hell. He's already seen my forbidden intimates. Why not?* I raised my head. "Thank you, Larry. That is sweet of you, and I will accept with gratitude."

"Great," he said. "The only other alternative was that I had to sleep on the couch down here." He smiled, put out his hand for my luggage, and rolled it alongside his to the elevator. Minnie was now dragging on the floor.

Our room was lovely. The window looked out onto the airport. The bathroom was quite large, and, as advertised, there were two comfy queen beds. We both stood in the room, unsure of what to do next.

"There's a great steakhouse downstairs right off the lobby. Would you like to join me for dinner?" Larry looked hopeful.

I looked out the window and saw that darkness was already descending, creating pools of swirling snow curtains in the airport lighting. The sight reminded my tummy that it had been hours since I last had a decent meal. "Larry," I responded, "I would love that." *So would my Visa card.*

He smiled and swept his arm toward the door. I smiled back and led the way.

Dinner was magnificent. We shared a wonderful bottle of wine and both had sizzling New York strips smothered in onions and mushrooms. The conversation was bright and delightful, words tumbling out between mouthfuls of prime beef. I felt comfortable with this man and started exploring ways to work him into my script as the romantic lead. He didn't fit any of the Hallmark criteria, but he was checking off a lot of my own personal boxes. He smiled a lot, and when he did, it lit up his face with an inner light. He was funny and personable and had a story to fit any occasion. He also was attentive and actually listened to me when I spoke.

"Do you have a dog?" I asked, trying to snug him into a Hallmark box.

"Nope. I travel too much to keep a pet."

"Any children?"

"Never been married."

"Own any tight jeans?"

"Umm now that's a strange question," he remarked with a look of confusion on his face.

"Sorry. I think the wine made me silly."

He grinned. "No no tight jeans," he answered.

*Damn! There goes the last shot to write him into the script.*

## Hallmark Christmas

# Chapter 3

I awoke the following morning with a gray light slipping in between the blinds. December twenty-third and it was still snowing. I could hear Larry on the phone in the bathroom. He shook his head as he walked out. "This storm is still bombing the Northeast; all eastbound flights are cancelled."

I noticed he was not in his pajamas; rather, he was in blue slacks and matching jacket. A glittering set of wings decorated his breast pocket. "Larry, is that a uniform?"

"It is."

"Are those pilot wings?"

"They are in fact. I'll be your pilot."

I found that astonishing. "Why were you sitting with the passengers on the flight here?"

"I had just completed a Hawaii charter and was deadheading back to Chicago to pick up your flight."

"Deadheading?"

"As an employee, I can fly for free if there is an open seat. It's called deadheading." He flipped up the blinds to let in some weak light and said, "Why don't you get dressed while I change back to civvies, and we can get some breakfast."

I grabbed a pair of jeans and a sweater and disappeared into the bathroom in ecstasy. *As a pilot Larry qualified as a romantic lead. It was even better than tight jeans. He was in!*

The sun poked holes in the storm clouds as we ate breakfast. By the time we stepped out for a breath of fresh air, the clouds had been shredded with slashes of blue, and the sun was raising a glitter field in the fallen snow. It was beautiful. I've lived in Southern California all my life and had never seen snow up close and personal. Once I revealed that to Larry he took over and soon had us making a snowman on the hotel grounds. Snow angels followed, and the day ended with a snowball melee with some of the other stranded passengers. The day passed in a happy blur, topped by another early dinner in the hotel restaurant. The roasted turkey was delightful.

As we sipped an after-dinner cocktail, Larry laid his hand on top of mine. I felt an electric current crackle between us. Our conversation slowed and softened until it seemed we were whispering so as not to share the moment with the other diners.

We finished our drinks and headed up to the room just as the last glow of the setting sun was painting burgundy clouds outside the window. Larry strolled up from behind and put his arms around me. "Beautiful, isn't it?" he murmured in my ear, then kissed me gently on the neck.

"Is this where the gentleman's promise ends?" I asked, turning to face him still in his embrace.

"Ah yes, there is that." He leaned in and kissed me on the lips. "I am showing great gentlemanly restraint," he whispered.

"You are." I kissed him right back. "A little less restraint might be nice," I said with almost no breath in my lungs.

A smile creased his face as he leaned in and kissed me again, full on – lips, tongue, and flaming passion in an embrace so tight I could barely breathe. My heart thundered in my chest, and I felt my legs going limp. The man could certainly kiss.

We were both frantic, tearing at buttons and zippers in an inferno of passion that grew as more and more skin was revealed.

We came up for air then kissed again. That was when the clothes started coming off. We were both frantic, tearing at buttons and zippers in an inferno of passion that grew as more and more skin was revealed. His shirt and my blouse fell together onto the floor. I ran my hands over his chest and arms, marveling at his muscled body while he slipped my bra off and cupped my breasts, making me sigh in pleasure. Moments later, we were naked, and he was lifting me into the bed.

The night passed in a delirium of pleasures. It had been a long time for me, and I simply couldn't get enough of him until exhaustion overwhelmed both of us. We lay spooned together as I fell asleep in an aura of joy.

A morning sunbeam woke me as I lay there tangled up in sheets, re-living the previous night. My phone was softly buzzing on the nightstand. As I picked it up to read the message, I glanced down to see my Minnie undies lying on the floor, right next to my Mickey bra.

Don't judge me

The text was from my girlfriend Joyce in Vermont. I read it twice.

I heard the shower stop, and a few minutes later Larry walked out of the bathroom butt naked and absolutely beautiful.

"I confirmed our flight for ten," he said, toweling off his hair. "I'm done in there if you wanna jump in the shower."

"Yeah, I need a shower after last night," I said and smiled up at him. "But I don't think I will be on that flight today."

"Oh? Why?"

"I got a text from Joyce. A corner of her roof collapsed yesterday from the snow load, and the house is unlivable right now. She's staying with friends, but I have nowhere to go. So I should probably just go back home."

That didn't seem to bother him. "You can go home or . . ."

"Or? Another or? Or what?"

"Or you can come home with me to New Hampshire."

"But . . ."

"Wait. Listen to me before you say something I might later regret."

I pulled the sheets around myself and sat up. "I'm listening."

"I have a really nice place right in the White Mountains with beautiful view, trees, mountains, snow. Everything you were talking about at dinner the other night. Come back with me. Today is Christmas Eve. You can spend it flying back to L.A., or you can spend it with my family at a special Christmas dinner. You would love it."

Larry walked to the bed, sat next to me, and put his arm around my shoulders. I was intimately aware of his nudity, but this wasn't sexy; it was comforting and sweet. "I promise you a better Christmas than you will get alone in L.A." He paused then added, "I can even renew my promise to be a gentleman if you wish."

That wasn't my wish.

## A Hallmark Christmas

# Chapter 4

The flight to Rutland, Vermont, was uneventful. We had a smaller jet than the one I took into Chicago. Larry managed to get me moved into first class where I had several cosmos to accompany me the whole way. I would have traded them all for Larry to be sitting next to me holding my hand. But he was up front flying the plane.

We landed with the tiniest of bumps. A few passengers got off, and a few more got on. Then we were back in the air on our way to Portsmouth, New Hampshire.

I picked it out easily by the silver duct tape covering the gaping hole in the corner. Larry met me then made a short call. A few minutes later, a golf cart arrived and whisked us off to a far corner of the airport.

We were dropped off in a huge hanger. "Where's your car?" I asked Larry.

"Car? What car? Our ride's right here," he said and pointed at a small four-person airplane. A mechanic had hooked a small tractor to the front wheel and was towing it outside the hanger.

*Oh dear God, the airplanes keep getting smaller.*

Larry loaded our luggage in the back then helped me into the right seat and nestled headphones and a seat restraint on me; then, he got in on the left side, belted himself in, and started up the engine. My hands were looking for something to grab, and it was obvious that the cosmos had worn off. I found the edge of his uniform jacket, crumpled it up in my fist, and held on tight.

We moved down the taxiway, got clearance from the tower, and turned onto the runway. Larry lined up with the centerline and pushed the throttle all the way in. The engine roared, and we accelerated down the runway. Larry pulled back on the yoke, and the nose came up; we were flying. I squealed—partly in fear, partly in exhilaration. This was nothing like flying in the big commercial planes.

We climbed up to four thousand feet and leveled off. "See that white tip of a mountain out there?" Larry asked.

"Yes."

"That's Mount Washington, the highest peak in the White Mountains. Give it ten minutes, and you'll be able to see all the White Mountain range." He removed my hand from the crumpled bunch of his jacket and held it in his own. "The family compound is just inside the foothills. Wait till you see that."

The White Mountains appeared like old worn teeth growing out of the ground, their sharp edges worn to nubs that still stuck up above our altitude. The whole range was covered with a smooth coating that looked like marshmallow fluff. Even the forests meandering through the valleys were encrusted with a thick glaze of immaculate white snow. It was gorgeous.

As we approached the foothills, Larry pulled off some power, and we began to descend toward a patch of cleared forest. I could see three houses backed up against the forest with a frozen river behind that. There was no airport in sight, yet we were almost falling out of the sky. The houses looked tiny but were growing larger by the second.

Larry let go of my hand and reached between the two seats to yank on a device that looked just like a hand brake on an old Volkswagen. I heard something clunk down below us.

"Skis," he said. "You can't land on wheels in that much snow. So we have skis attached to the landing gear. I just lowered them. We'll ski our way in." He pulled the throttle all the way back, and the engine quieted down. We dropped toward the ground.

I could now clearly see the three houses and a long white expanse of snow in front of us. He gave my hand a friendly pat and grasped the yoke with both hands. I immediately grabbed his jacket and held on for dear life.

"Don't be afraid," he said. "I do this all the time."

We slid down onto the snow and, to my surprise, slid smoothly and quietly to a stop two-thirds of the way down the snow-coated runway. I could breathe again.

Larry throttled back up and moved us toward a hanger attached to the last house. I noticed that all three houses had hangers attached. *The whole family flies?*

At the hanger he shut off the engine, told me to stay put, and disappeared into the building, reappearing on a lawn tractor. He hooked the tractor to the airplane and towed it into the hanger then helped me out of the plane.

"Welcome to my home," he said and bowed, sweeping his hand toward the house in front of us. The spectacular, two-story, log cabin glowed a golden maple in the declining sunlight. It was the perfect picture of my intended Hallmark hideout.

"Larry, it's beautiful."

"Come on in. Let's get you freshened up before dinner."

I gasped when we got inside. The house was rustic and simply decorated, but the simplicity added to a rural magnificence. High ceilings and massive timbers gave it the feel of a cathedral.

Larry dragged our suitcases into the master suite. "There are three bedrooms; you can choose any one you want."

"This will do nicely," I said and leaned in and kissed him. He nodded, smiled, and left to make some phone calls. I got my travel kit out of the suitcase and primped a little, restoring my make-up and lipstick, then changed into a dress more appropriate for a dinner.

By the time we walked back outside, the sun had dropped below the trees, lighting the top of Mount Washington with a fiery orange glow. Now it was time to "meet the folks."

A little flip of nerves rippled through my tummy. *Did I belong here?*

## A Hallmark Christmas

## Chapter 5

Larry's family proved just as wonderful and friendly as Larry himself. His parents, John and Dolores, retired young after making a fortune in commercial real estate. They bought this land, built all three houses for themselves and their kids, and settled into the joys of family. Their daughter, Pam, was married to a lawyer and had two young children. Larry remained unmarried and childless, a situation they were anxious to alter.

The whole family had gathered in the main house for their Christmas feast, and I became the center of attention.

"Larry's never brought a friend home for Christmas," Dolores whispered. "You must be special."

I blushed at that. "Dolores, he's kinda special to me too," I replied.

"It's Dee to you, Kathy, and it pleases me that you like my boy. I kinda like him too." The dinner was sumptuous and overflowed with conversation and laughter. I felt such a part of it all.

After the table was cleared and the dishes piled in the kitchen for later attention, we all gathered around the magnificent Christmas tree in the family room. Dee handed out gifts from a pile on the floor, ensuring that every family member got one. "Kathy," she said, "There's one here for you too." She handed me a small box wrapped in foil and ribbons.

"I didn't expect. . . how did you. . ." I fumbled opening the box.

"Larry called and asked if he could bring you. Of course we said yes, and I added a trip into town for a welcome gift for you."

I teared up, looked at Larry who shrugged and smiled, then had to wipe my eyes to see the gift. It was a stunning set of silver wings with gold inlay on a silver chain.

"We wanted you to remember that strange family with all those airplanes," Dee added.

I embarrassed myself by wiping away the tears that flowed like two creeks on my cheeks. "T- Thank you and I could never forget this family. You've made me feel like a family member."

I had been sitting on the floor and stood up, clutching the necklace. "Excuse me a minute," I muttered and escaped to the bathroom to dab at my tears.

When I returned, everyone acted as though nothing had happened. Larry motioned me over to the couch, held up his hands, and pulled me into a cuddle. "You are something special, ya know that?"

"Your mom said the same thing."

"My mom is a wise woman."

We stayed for awhile, bathing in the glow of family. I helped Pam wash the dinner dishes; then, Larry and I returned to his house. We had an evening cocktail then crawled into bed—together. Unlike our crazy sexual explosion back at the hotel, we made love slowly and tenderly, adrift on a warm sea of desire, then cuddled ourselves to a blissful sleep. I woke once through the night, felt his arms around me, felt his breath on my neck, and whispered, "I love you" then drifted back to sleep.

Christmas Day. My family used to celebrate Christmas, but my parents live in Florida now I live in L.A., and my sister ran off with a trapeze flyer from the circus. Yeah, really, a trapeze flyer of all things. So, it has been a while since I last enjoyed a traditional Christmas. The Cummings family celebrates Christmas with all the pomp and ceremony it deserves, fabulous meal, gifts, lights, and laughter. It was the best Christmas I have had since I was ten.

Mr. Cummings—he said to call him John—rented a huge sleigh pulled by two massive horses, and after dinner we all piled in, snuggled down under heavy furs and had a wonderful sleigh ride through the forest. It was magical. The day ended too soon as did each day until my week was eaten up by endless delights, both in and out of bed.

I went skiing for the first time, and Larry was kind enough to stay with me on the bunny hill. We had snowmobile rides and soaring airplane tours over the White Mountains. I ice skated on a hidden forest pond, rode horseback to a saloon in the nearby town of Jackson, and actually tied our horses to a hitching post while we went inside for a glass of wine. It was arguably the best week of my life. But nothing can last forever.

New Year's Eve. Larry and I spent it together at his house, watching the ball drop in New York. We cuddled on the couch, sipping the last of the evening wine. "Larry," I said, kissing him, "I've been here a week and it's time I go back home." I had all the background I needed to write my script, and it was getting hard to justify staying in New Hampshire any longer.

"Can you book me a flight back to LAX?" I asked.

"Sure, I can, but why would I?"

"Because I asked you to."

"Not good enough. I don't want you to go."

I started to tear up. That seems to happen a lot around this man. "But, sweetie, I gotta go home. All my stuff is there."

"It's only stuff. I'm here. Stay here. Make this home."
He didn't understand. I had to go home.

\*\*\*

January twenty-first. I check my email every day, expecting a response from Hallmark. Nothing yet, but I smile whenever I think of New Hampshire. It was an amazing Christmas, one I will never forget. I top off my gas tank, get back into my car, and pull out onto I-95. Boston is my next stop. From there New Hampshire is just one more day. The car is loaded with my stuff, and my heart is filled with the memory of Larry's parting words— "I love you, Kathy. Come live with me."

Sounds like a plan to me. I hope I packed my Disney underwear.

Flash Prompt:  Murder Most Foul

## The Soul Seeker
### by Beverly Jackson

    The knife sliced deep and smooth across her supple neck.  So simple.  He lowers her body gently to the floor.  He cradles her head lovingly as he examines her face, a face petrified in disbelief.  He studies her eyes, the window to her soul, until life ebbs away.  Only then does euphoria fill him; the demons relax and sleep ensues.  This is the only time he feels normal.  It is the same every time.

    Repetition creates perfection.  This is Mr. Smith's mantra: "One little mistake can cost me the loss of everything that makes me whole."  Ever vigilant, he pursues his life's work.  He never kills in the same place twice, never favors a certain type.  All that matters is the blissful release of peace and the dreamless sleep that follows.

    A new city has been chosen in a new state.  Mr. Smith feels the anxiety bubbling inside.  It's time.  Tonight he hunts.  Waiting patiently outside a bar near closing time, he watches the patrons leave.  A lone female walks toward her car.  Now.  Silently, he approaches from behind.  His left arm encircles the small figure.  Her futile efforts make Mr. Smith smile.  At the same moment, his right arm extends, his hand holding the knife of choice, swiftly finishing the job.  Staring into her eyes, deep pools of blue, he feels the warmth flowing through him, and his soul is fulfilled once more.

Flash Prompt: Murder Most Foul

## Skeletal Rage

by Jane Schopen

I have hiked the desert
and paddled silver lakes,
climbed forests of mountains.
Now darkness overtakes.

Shadows close upon me
like burglars in the night.
Unstoppable, they plunder
though I tried to live life right.

I am angry. I am lessened.
There is no going gentle.
I mourn time and activity
once so fundamental.

Prideful, wounded animal
I shun assist and solace.
Only take this mortal dust
to its worldly terminus.

Fiery wrath and ashes,
what will remain to give.
May they fuel earth's roil
continuing to live.

Toss me to the white-hot sands,
wind-whipped and severe.
Float me atop waterways,
storm-tossed and unclear.

  Iy me on the mountaintop,
    child of cataclysm.
   I'll rage ever upward
   with one final criticism.

  If y bones could spell it out--
  MURDER, most offending.
    I am not ungrateful.
   I just hate the ending.

Flash prompt: Murder Most Foul

## Delayed Revenge
### by Claudia Haeckel

When Berta met Jimmy, he asked her, "What's your dream home like?"

Berta replied, "I want to live far away from everyone. When I see a car on my road, I'll know they are coming to see me, because no one else lives there. If someone's coming, they're welcome because I invited them. It's very quiet and peaceful."

*****

A divorced single mother of six-year-old Paulette, Berta worked in a busy pediatric clinic. They lived in a nice apartment complex. Berta felt lucky to have found this place. Jan and Ron, the couple next door had fallen in love with Paulette and baby-sat her while Berta worked.

Two months before Berta met Jimmy, the man she had been seeing for a year decided, without any input from her, that they should get married. Even thinking about it gave her panic attacks. Berta realized she didn't want to marry Art. What she didn't need was another man who didn't think she could make any major decisions on her own. She overcame her terror, and after calming down, and really thinking about it, she decided she didn't want to remarry anyone.

Art was confident. He believed Berta loved him and was, as he told her "just confused". Art continued to call and stop by with some small offering. He stopped at fruit stands and brought them fruit. He shopped for special school supplies for Paulette. He made every effort to be helpful and kind. Nothing he did moved Berta in his direction.

After work one afternoon, Berta was next door picking up Paulette, when Art pulled into Berta's driveway blocking her car. She could see him from Jan's small porch, but was sure he didn't see her. Berta ducked back into the corner. Jan raised her eyebrows and tried to suppress a smile.

Jan pushed the door open and said, "Come on in. Have a glass of iced tea. Is it okay if Paulette has a couple of cookies so close to dinner?"

"Sure, nothing ruins that girl's appetite."

Jan's husband, Ron, came into the room. He laughed and said, "Looks like you don't want company tonight."

"Nope, I'm tired. I just want to fix dinner for me and Paulette and go to bed as soon as she's asleep.

Ron said, "You know you're never going to get rid of him, seems like he's over there two or three times a week at dinner time. I know you're feeding him. Why should he leave? At least when you were a couple, he was buying dinner and doing more than buying Paulette a couple of barrettes or a pencil. Don't feel guilty that you don't want to marry him. The way things are now, you may as well be married. You need to start dating. And--stop feeding him! Men are like stray dogs. If you feed them, they'll never leave."

"He's right," Jan said.

"Maybe." Berta sighed.

"Maybe nothing, you're in a rut," Ron said. "By the way, Art just left. He hung around, probably trying to figure out why your car was there, and you weren't."

Ron was interrupted by loud banging on the door, and yelled "Come on in Jimmy." Then smiled and said, "I ordered pizza as soon as I saw you both sit down. Figured it was the only way I would get something to eat before bedtime. It's O.K. if you two talk all night. Jimmy and I can keep busy. Oh Berta, this is James Riley. Jimmy this is our neighbor Berta."

Jimmy was immediately taken with Berta's heavy shoulder length honey-blond hair and her warm flawless skin. His first thought, *She's so touchable. I want to touch her*. As he gazed into her dark brown eyes, they talked late into the night, he knew, she was who he wanted to marry. Ron and Jan had taken Paulette into the living room to watch a Disney movie. Later Jimmy carried a sleeping Paulette next door and left after asking Berta to dinner that week-end.

Berta smiled into his clear blue eyes, "I'd like that. Ron said I should start dating."

Jimmy darted back to Ron's and told him "I want you to be my best man. I'm going to marry Berta. Ahem, don't say anything I haven't asked her yet." It didn't take him long; five months later they were married.

*****

Twenty-nine years later, after Jimmy retired, they started looking for homes with land in the Idyllwild-Anza Valley area. They stopped at a real-estate office on Hwy-371. Darla, the only agent at the office, was standing outside smoking. Annoyed by the intrusion she brushed off the ash, pinching the burnt end to be sure it was out and put it back into the Camel pack. She wore skintight jeans and well-worn dirty cowboy boots. The dusty ground surrounding her was covered with butts. The smell of stale cigarettes floated around Darla as she led them into the rustic building. Her long kinky brown hair streaked with grey was unrestrained.

When a breeze floated through the window behind her, her hair came alive with movement, blowing its scent, and something else, an unknown odor, across the desk to Jimmy and Berta. Jimmy reverted to mouth-breathing to avoid the smell. Berta's eyes watered.

Jimmy said, "We want to look at some homes with land and possibly some outbuildings. We'd like it off the highway away from traffic."

Darla said, "I got lots to show you. You have to follow me. My back seat is full of chicken feed and wire."

Once they pulled onto the highway behind Darla's dusty, dented, old rust colored Mercury Marquis and were on their way, Jimmy turned to Berta and said, "Chicken Shit."

"What.?"

"Chicken Shit. That's Darla's mystery perfume."

"Probably."

Jimmy poked Berta in the ribs and said, "OK, let's find your dream home."

*****

They both loved their five-acre farm. They planted a nice family orchard that now was bearing fruit and nuts. The vegetable plot was flourishing. Berta's lilac and rose bushes, loaded with blooms, smelled heavenly. Jimmy had the huge high-end metal shop, the reason he wanted this piece of property. It had been a repossession and they weren't going to look inside because it was too small. To build the shop would have cost three times what they paid for their place. Darla their realtor had known Jimmy would love the shop.

*****

Berta sighed, shook out a capsule of gabapentin, tossed it into her mouth and washed it down with water. Jimmy looked away "It's OK Honey, that's what the pills are for. If you're having a bad night, maybe it will help you get some rest, a little sleep will do you a lot of good."

Berta snapped back "Sleep with drugs is different from real sleep. I wake up numb and stupid, not rested"

Jimmy looked at the floor, bit his lip, took a deep breath, exhaled, and walked into the living room. Berta came from a family rife with substance abuse. She never drank or smoked and took exceptional care of her health so she would never have to deal with prescription drugs, the horrid side effects or the temptation of addiction.

It had been four years since they were rammed from behind by a drunk driver. John Greene didn't have a license due to three previous drunk driving convictions. They were almost home. The closest stores were forty-five minutes away. It had been a long day, the trunk and back seat were full of Christmas gifts and needed groceries, in a few more minutes they would be home. They were on the last little stretch of the two-lane paved road, the car in front of them stopped for oncoming traffic to make a left turn. Jimmy slowed to a stop and glanced in the rear-view mirror. The new gray Ford Focus wasn't slowing down, the car in front of him was still waiting for a break in the oncoming cars.

Jimmy yelled, "Shit! There's nowhere to go." The side of the road had only a foot and a half of water-logged dirt from recent rain and melted snow before a deep ditch. Berta turned and looked at the car barreling down on them. She could see the driver's face, it was a total blank, no expression whatsoever. At that moment their car jerked forward, the car in front had begun to turn and Jimmy squeezed by. They were picking up speed, there was nothing on the road ahead.

Berta looked back and said, "He's way back there, looks like he isn't moving."

Jimmy let up on the gas, then checked the rear-view mirror. "Oh my God. He's coming right at us." Trying to outrun the crazed driver, Jimmy had the car up to eighty when he hit them. Everything went quiet, the car was air-borne, they came down hard in the empty oncoming lane. Both cars had come to a stop.

Jimmy looked at Berta "Are you okay?"

"I think so."

"How about you?"

"Not sure, but we're lucky to be alive. Call 911."

Jimmy went to check on the guy in the grey Ford. The driver, who reeked of alcohol, looked at Jimmy with glazed eyes through the open window, and took off, hitting Jimmy in the arm with the side mirror. He nearly hit Jimmy's Chevy on the passenger side. Jimmy ran back to the car and followed him off the paved road onto some of the worst roads in the area. The Chevy was banging and scraping bottom on the rutted road.

Berta was unable to get 911 on her cell, so she dialed their nearest neighbor and told them all that was happening. The neighbors were on their way home from shopping, Myrna put her phone on speaker, Joe had the 911 dispatcher listening on his phone. Berta was giving their location and an incomplete license number and the car color, make and model to 911 by relay. The dispatcher asked Berta to hang up and said she would call Berta back. She told them, "Stay where you are, or go home if your car can make it home. Do not try and make contact with the other driver. Everybody up there has a gun. A deputy is on his way, he will be there within forty-five or fifty minutes. I will stay on the line until I know you are safe."

*****

As a result of the accident Jimmy had shoulder surgery and suffered with severe headaches along with back and neck pain. Berta had the headaches and neck pain. She also contracted shingles brought on by stress. Dr. Burns said it was the worst case he'd ever seen or heard of. The Urgent Care doctor prescribed two wrong medications, which didn't help, but gave her lingering intestinal problems. She was still having those problems along with being one of those unlucky few who never get relief from the nerve pain of shingles. The formerly active and healthy couple were finding it difficult maintaining their dream home. They were tired and in pain most of the time. Since the accident Berta thought of their retirement farm as paradise lost.

*****

Berta slathered Vaseline on the barrel of her 357 Ruger. She wrapped the barrel with a small piece of cheese cloth covered with tinfoil. Berta hated to do this to her favorite gun.

She layered men's work clothes over her shorts and tank top, slipped on a pair of tired, used-up sneakers, covered her hair with a bandana, and put on a pair of welding glasses. Thanks to Covid-19 everyone is expected to wear a facemask. Berta carefully placed the loaded gun under the driver's seat, got into her old Jeep Cherokee and went hunting.

Almost daily his prey was able to hitch a ride from the Casino on the Highway to the rutted rural dirt road. While his girlfriend was in the hospital, he trashed her new Ford Focus in the accident. City people in nice cars didn't come down our roads and most locals wouldn't give him a lift. There he was drunk as always. John Greene couldn't believe his luck. He was asleep or passed-out within minutes of climbing into the passenger seat of Berta's Jeep.

He awoke, focused on the barrel of Berta's gun. He begged, and cried, his face a disgusting mess of snot and tears. The smell of booze and body odor tinged with fear, made Berta gag. She ordered him out and it got worse, he soiled himself. She took him through the back entrance of the hog farm, dense with scrub oak and grease wood. Urging John on with a large sharp stick. They pushed through to an area tramped down by an animal. She pulled an oversized plastic bag from a pocket made him undress and fill the bag with his clothing. "Bend over. Grab your ankles."

It was as messy as Berta imagined; the gunshot was muffled.

*****

Berta took off the bandana, face mask, the old sneakers and the men's work clothes and put them in with John's belongings. She dropped the oversized plastic bag at the dump transfer station.

When Berta slipped into the laundry room through the back door, she stripped, placing everything she wore in the washer on the longest cycle with cold water and the whole bottle of peroxide. She stood there, naked in the laundry room and cleaned Jimmy's welding glasses and her beloved gun using old rags, paper towels and pipe cleaners. Berta built a fire in the fireplace, waited until she was sure all the rags and paper towels were gone. She was in the mist of a long hot shower when Jimmy came home from his appointment at the VA Hospital. Berta stepped out of the shower, she felt Jimmy looking at her, she looked into Jimmy's loving eyes, and relaxed. She smiled and gave him a big hug.

"How was your appointment?"

"Good. Real good. The x-rays and lab work show improvement. "He held up his welding glasses, "And someone cleaned my stuff for me."

"Well, I used them to do some dirty work outside today. I got a lot done. It feels good to clean out all that garbage, it's gone, hauled to the dump. It makes me feel like I accomplished something today. I feel good."

Jimmy smiled, hugged her tighter, and gave her a long soft kiss.

# The Chat
## by Jim Veary

I was in the middle of raging through a teenage hissy fit because my mother wouldn't let me have the car, and my girlfriend, Maureen, was leaving for her family's spring vacation in Florida when God walked into my bedroom. I didn't actually see him enter. There was no knock, no sound at all. He might have walked through the door or through the wall for all I knew, but he calmly strode to my bed and sat down at the foot. I saw the mattress compress and heard the squeak of the springs, so I knew he was real.

"Who the hell are you?" I asked, brandishing a table lamp like a club.

"You can put that down, son," he said. "I'm not going to hurt you. I'm God," he added in a voice that projected peace in the face of my sudden fear. "I'm from the good place. You know, kinda the opposite of hell."

"Huh?"

"God, you know—the creator of the universe, the Supreme Being, the man with the plan."

"Yeah, I get it. I get it." I instantly calmed down then, just as quickly, felt an overwhelming sense of guilt creep up my neck and flush my face. He wasn't dressed like God, no robes, no glowing halo, no flowing beard. He wore gnarly tattered Converse High Tops, green Bermudas, and a yellow Polo shirt. The only thing that matched the God image was the serenity that flooded his face and seemed to light up the room. But despite the lack of obvious proof, I believed him, of course. You can't go around denying God. I scanned the room. There were no attending angels, no saints following in an honor guard, no orchestra playing Handel's *Messiah*, no Mormon Tabernacle Choir singing his praises. Just God. . . in my room. . . on my bed.. . Oh boy!

I was in deep shit!

"If this is about not going to church, I can explain. . ."

"Nope. Go to church; don't go to church. At your age, it doesn't really matter. I'm not overly insistent on the whole worship thing, at least not for young people. There will be plenty of time and need for that when you get older."

"But my mom makes me."

"Your mom is giving you a solid foundation, something you will need to build your own life. If the foundation is good, then the life you build on it will be just fine."

"Then this is about Maureen and me. . ."

"Wrong again, but nice try. I made you the way you are—the horniness, the wet dreams, the endless thoughts of sex. It's okay. It's all part of the design. It was originally for the survival of the species, but your media has blown it all way out of proportion. Just be careful not to abuse it. It'll calm down eventually."

"So, should I confess my sins?"

"What sins? You're seventeen years old. You haven't lived long enough to really sin."

"Then why are you here?"

"I had some time. I thought we could use a good talk." He patted the bed beside him and I joined him.

"Am I in trouble?" I asked.

"No. Why do you ask?" God replied.

"Well God doesn't normally drop into your bedroom for a little talk. I would think you'd have more important things to do."

"Ahhh, but there again you are wrong. Each soul in my universe is important in its own way. I am always whispering in your ear. But I find that few people actually listen. So I decided to do it in the flesh. Pretty hard to ignore me now, isn't it?"

"Oh yeah."

"Good advice is almost certain to be ignored, but that's no reason not to give it. You and your sister Angeline have an astonishing future ahead of you. You will do great things."

"Like what?"

"I can't tell you that. It might scare you at this point. But don't be afraid of being afraid. Sometimes the one thing you need for growth is the one thing you are most afraid to do. That's my first and best advice. Believe in yourself and trust your instincts. You won't regret walking the path you will be taking. Believe me, I know."

"You don't make it sound easy."

"Life's challenges never are. When I think of you, I think of many of the kids today. You are stuck. It's basic physics. An object in motion tends to stay in motion, and an object not in motion tends to, well, not leave his room for the better part of the day. You sit here and worry about what tomorrow will bring. Don't bring tomorrow's troubles into today. Today has enough troubles of its own."

"But. . ."

"No but about it. Trust me on this. I have one last piece of advice. Stand tall, be a man, and do what has to be done. Much will be expected of you."

We talked on a bit, mostly about my father abandoning us years ago and the strength of my mother in holding the family together. He said Mom had given me everything I needed to face life as a man. That made me feel good.

I heard the crash of a dish downstairs and God stood up.

"It's time," he said. "Take your cell phone and call 911."

"911?"

"Yes. Tell them to send an ambulance to this address."

"Ambulance?" I said as I picked up my phone.

"Tell them your mother is having a heart attack."

"Oh dear God," I muttered as I spoke into the phone.

God smiled. "'Dear God?' I kinda like that. It's certainly an improvement over 'Who the hell are you?' Now, let's go downstairs, and I will talk you through performing CPR. You will be just fine and so will your mother in time."

I stumbled down the stairs and into my unknown future, made all the more unknown because I now knew that I actually had a future.

# Do Not Mourn Me
## by Pat Leso

Do not mourn me now that I'm gone.

Embrace the memories we shared.

Remember walks along the beach,

The surf and sand between your toes.

Relive the camping trips and sleeping under stars.

Treasure the sweet moonlight kisses and

Ice cream, watermelon, barbecues,

Seashells, sunsets, swimming, and tans.

Look back at boating and fishing trips,

Iced tea at the poolside with friends,

Cut off jeans, tank tops, and bikinis.

Embrace those memories.

I'll always be in your thoughts and dreams.

Remember me and know I'll always return.

Your friend forever,

Summer

## Crow's Funeral
### by Claudia Haeckel

Georgia shivered in the hot Arizona sun, wrapping her arms around her body. Eyes transfixed, wide open, alert, and unblinking as she stared at the large black crows on her wrought iron fence. The crows, five coal-black birds, looked like the darkest of winged shadows, their beaks and legs indistinguishable in their darkness. Only their eyes, like black jewels seemed to be staring back at Georgia.

Georgia explained to her neighbor Pat, "They can tell people apart, you know. Crows can distinguish facial features. They can tell one person from another. They can tell the difference between a gun and another metal object, like a rake handle. Crows transmit this information by squawking signals if there's danger. If a sentry makes a mistake he's put on trial and sometimes executed for his mistake. They have an intelligent system of government. Crows are social birds, who use tools. They care for their sick and injured. They hold funerals."

"Really?"

"Oh yes, really."

Intrigued, Pat asked Georgia, who was still in a stare-down with the crows, "You seem to have a lot of uncommon knowledge about crows. Did you research them as part of one of your special projects for your class?"

"Yes, I did a lot of research on them after the funeral."

"The funeral?" Pat questioned.

"The crow's funeral."

Georgia and her husband were winter residents in Lake Havasu City. She was a retired fourth-grade school teacher, her husband Darryl, a successful retired dentist, the eldest child of a large family, was raised on a farm in Washington state. Darryl was happiest when working outdoors in his garden.

"Days before Darryl shot the crow in the rows of corn, he'd tried everything to scare the crows away, but nothing worked. They were destroying the whole garden, the corn being their favorite. After he shot the crow, he pounded a stake into the ground and nailed the crow to it."

Never taking her eyes away from the birds Georgia continued: "It was just before dawn, in the early morning quiet, the atmosphere seemed to change. Eerie, flapping and whooshing noises, sounding like a sudden wind storm erupted, then just as quickly the sounds stopped. I went to the window, as the sun was rising. The garage and shop roof were black with crows, the big blue spruce trees covered with crows, the fence covered with crows. Once the sun cleared the horizon, they all began calling, a hoarse, coarse, cawing, caucus. It was terrifying. It's still so vivid for me. The racket was awful. I became sick to my stomach. They carried on for forty-five minutes, then suddenly stopped. Whooshing and flapping, they were gone and never returned that summer. I'm going inside"

We retreated into the house, the birds still watching. They seemed to be glaring at us.

# Death Be Not Prod

by Tim Montbriand

"Raymond Jenks, get your nose out of that stupid tabloid and do some work around here. You don't have an inquiring mind; if you did, you'd ask your wife if you could help her keep this house from falling down around us."

"I'm sorry, Gildea. I know you're a good wife, and you're right. I should help out a little more. Just let me finish my research here before I tackle your chore list."

"Research, ha! You're an ignorant and lazy sonofabitch." She glared at Ray, and one side of her upper lip curled up like that of a crazed and contemptuous Elvis as it always did when she was angry.

She was wrong. Ray did have an inquiring mind. He was reading the popular tabloid for its two fascinating stories about near-death experiences. Many of the near deceased later recounted how they were strongly drawn to a bright light, the inference being that the light was a heavenly light beckoning them. Ray didn't deny or doubt the inference—he was a religious person who believed in the afterlife—but he was more inclined to believe that the suffering patients in their fight for life were struggling toward the lights over the operating table.

He had brought up the subject on occasion with Gildea. "You know those people who have been pronounced dead for a short time and come alive again? Have you ever wondered what that's like?"

"I don't give a shit about that," she said, her lip curling in disgust. "What I want to know is if your dead ass is alive and gonna get some work done around here instead of sittin' reading bullshit."

"Thanks, honey," Ray muttered under his breath as he discarded the pandering, populist tabloid. He was interested in a subject more intriguing than near-death experiences, namely just-after-death experiences. That compulsive interest had begun with his readings of Emily Dickinson's poems back in high school. Dickinson wrote several poems describing conscious moments after death: a person hearing the last sighs of mourners and a buzzing fly attracted to her now dead body;[1] a woman being driven by Death in a carriage that takes her past the mound that will be her grave as the carriage's horses pull her inexorably toward "eternity,"[2] a person who hears mourners treading over her grave.[3]

Ray had also read extensively about the French Revolution guillotine experiments and was both intrigued and horrified by the account of a French scientist who, sentenced to death by guillotine, asked his assistant to observe whether or not the scientist's severed head in the executioner's basket could blink to signal that his brain still functioned. According to legend, the scientist blinked fifteen to twenty times.

In another account, Jean-Paul Marat, a very popular French Revolutionist was murdered in his bathtub by Charlotte Corday. When Corday was guillotined, the executioner held up Corday's severed head and slapped her face. Corday, again according to legend, turned her head, her cheeks reddening in outrage, and gave the executioner a nasty look.

Ray's favorite account, though, was about two rivals in the French Revolution. When their severed heads plopped into the basket below the guillotine, one bit the other on the cheek fiercely, and they had to be pulled apart.

Ray tried again to get Gildea interested in his avocation and his research. "Hey, Gildea, come here a minute." Gildea walked into the room looking annoyed that she had been so peremptorily summoned. She wore rubber gloves and had a wet paintbrush in her hand.

"What the hell do you want?" she snarled.

"I've been reading some interesting stuff. How long do you think the brain continues to function after the heart stops beating?"

"That's a question that has always puzzled me, Ray darling. I was pondering that very thing while I was painting the kitchen. I phrased the question a little differently than you did though. I was seriously asking myself, 'How long does the heart keep functioning after the brain is dead?' Your brain is dead from thinking about nothing but death, and your heart and my heart sure ain't workin'; there's no love here. Do me this one favor, butthead, cut that elm tree limb hanging by the side door of the garage. I can hardly get past it when I pull the lawn mower out."

Gildea stalked out of the room, her lip curled up as if reaching for her eye. When she left, Ray resumed his musings about how strange it is that life's two most important experiences, birth and death, are never really experienced.

We can't remember our births at all, and if we remember anything about our infancy, it's a fog of innocence and wonder, our souls entering our bodies from some limbo-like existence, "trailing clouds of glory" as Wordsworth so aptly described it. And in death, why does consciousness cease if there is an afterlife? We should be able to experience the transition fully.

Frustrated, he went out to the garage, got his chainsaw, started it roaring, and cut down the limb of the elm tree, which was extremely thick and dropped heavily to the ground. He noticed too late that Gildea had come out to shout directions at him. She lay pinned beneath the limb's trunk.

The ambulance was quick to respond to his call and took Gildea to the emergency room, where Ray sat by her side, a dutiful husband watching the green screen monitoring vital signs. When the heartbeat flatlined, the doctor walked in saying, "I'm sorry, Mr. Jenks, she's gone."

Ray bent over Gildea's ear and whispered, "I love you, honey. I wish you hadn't tried to help me with that tree but had let me do the work on my own as always." He saw Gildea's lip curl up severely.

The doctor said, "In death, the body's nerves and muscles often spasm. It's all right, Mr. Jenkins."

[1] "I heard a fly buzz when I died"
[2] "Because I could not stop for death"
[3] "I felt a funeral in my brain"

Flash prompt: Haunted

## Duffy Dawg's Ball
by Claudia Haeckel

The music played "The Farmer in the Dell" then "Ring around the Rosie" and, after a slight pause, "Mary had a little Lamb," our all-time favorite. It always drove Duffy wild when I sang that one to him. He was such a little clown. I picture him holding the ball aloft by the rough chewed-up ridge around the middle. If the music stopped, he set the ball down and pushed one of the buttons. I believe he knew the one in the middle played "Mary had a Little Lamb." The ball, a Fisher-Price baby toy, was heavy and taller than his sleek little black and tan dachshund hard-body. Duffy loved all balls, but hands down, this was his all-time favorite.

I had eighteen wonderful years of love and devotion from Duffy. We all miss him. His ball is still in the toy box. Jackson, our other dog, never cared for balls, so the music toy hasn't been played with for a couple of weeks. I hear the music in my head; it never stops. I've been hearing it for about ten days.

Mike stopped playing solitaire, a quizzical look on his face. He went to the front windows and looked outside. Curious, I followed him. He opened the front door and hurried down the drive, stepped into the street and looked both ways, put his hands in his pocket, shrugged his shoulders, and came back to me standing in the open doorway.

"I knew it was too good to be true," he said. "I still hear it. I think it's an ice cream truck."

"You hear it?" I asked. "It's Duffy's ball...listen."

Together we walked to the basket we use as a toy chest for the dogs. There it was, nested in a corner. The music never stopped. Mike looked at me.

"It's Duffy, I asked him to let me know he's okay, if there's anything after this life. You know he'd do anything for me." Mike squeezed my hand.

Then, the music stopped.

Flash prompt: Haunted

## Warrior's Lament
### by Karen VanderJagt

The bullet has hit Brian in the temple. Brain matter flies through the air to strike my face. I run to his side and kneel.

Then I wake up.

The dream is always the same. Sweat covers my brow, and I get up to run to the bathroom to wash the memory from my face. When will the dreams stop? Tonight it was Brian. Tomorrow, maybe the dream will be Tommy.

I stumble into the kitchen and grab a beer from the fridge. The clock says four AM. Who the hell cares? Collapsing on the recliner, I take a long pull from my beer and focus on the cool flow as it moistens my dry throat. My eyes close.

"Honey?" Janet's soft voice calls from the doorway. "Another dream?"

I shrug.

"Please go to the doctor." Janet lays a hand on my shoulder. "Get help."

I shrug.

She sighs.

After Janet returns to bed, I finish my beer and contemplate the day. It'll be just like yesterday. Tomorrow night will be just like tonight. I open the drawer and look at my gun. I feel like I'm walking through black mud that's trying to swallow me. The time has come. What will I choose?

"Please come back to bed," Janet calls from the bedroom.

I close the drawer. My wife doesn't deserve to see what I have seen.

I go back to bed. Janet pulls back the covers, and I lay my head on her shoulder.

"I love you," she whispers.

Flash prompt: Surprisingly It's Okay

## Dropouts and Losers

by Jane Schopen

"That's pathetic," Ashly said to her friend Trisha sitting next to her on the bleachers.

"Wha...?"

"Jill and her kids over there at the track."

Trisha looked at the adjoining field where a woman walked a dog, two boys played catch, and a girl performed a stringer of cartwheels. She glanced over at her own two boys sitting in the baseball dugout.

"I mean," Ashly continued, "you know, her husband left her, and she had to take the kids out of the activities they love."

"I talked to her at the store the other day," said Trisha. "She actually seems quite happy, said she had to pull the plug on mixed martial arts, cheer, and gymnastics because the credit card was maxed out."

"Yeah, but why baseball and soccer too? They're not that expensive," said Ashly, gesturing toward the game in front of them.

"Seriously? All the away-game weekends and food on the run really add up for us, not to mention the time suck—my life feels crazy! When I'm not in the car, I'm rushing to do my house stuff, making sure everyone's homework gets done, and trying to grab a little sleep. Jill said they have an actual schedule at her house now, and they're all a lot nicer to each another. I'm jealous."

Both women fell silent for a minute as they watched Jill's family play.

"Looks like Jill lost weight," Ashly observed.

"Twenty pounds she said."

"Well, shit..." sighed Ashly.

## Go Greyhound
### by Tim Montbriand

When Johnny Starzky was fourteen, his father brought home a player piano. The whole family took turns pumping the pedals and delighting in the ragtime sounds the piano produced, but they soon tired of the novelty. Johnny, though, liked to watch the keys being depressed. After a time, he detected a pattern in the lower keys and was able to play a rudimentary version of a left-hand "vamp." He learned the melody by ear, put the left-hand and right-hand parts together and had a passable version of the song.

Once Johnny's father heard Johnny play that song, he would announce to every visitor, "You gotta hear Johnny play the piano." Johnny would always demur, saying things like, "I'm just learning; I'm not that good." After being coaxed and cajoled, though, he would play, and the praise that followed, genuine or not, made his heart swell. He wanted more.

On his sixteenth birthday, Johnny received a cheap, nylon-stringed guitar. Johnny loved it. It was so much more intimate than the piano; he could cradle it in his arms, and the sounds seemed to emanate from his own body. He started playing popular songs and singing along. He had a mellow voice and projected well, not "Vienna Boys' Choir" pure but pleasing enough. In the ensuing years, he was invited to many parties and was always asked to bring his guitar. As was his way, when he was asked to start playing, he would always act a bit reluctant until the audience became insistent.

Johnny performed with some local musicians, but the ad hoc groups were never talented enough to produce what Johnny wanted most: praise and adulation. At nineteen, he knew that he would have to go it alone. He left a short note to his parents and bought a one-way ticket to Nashville.

Johnny's friend Mike drove him through the darkened caverns of downtown Detroit to the Greyhound bus station. "I still don't know what the hell you're doing," Mike said.

"Just followin' a dream, Mike. Thanks for the ride. I'll be in touch."

Johnny got out of the car with a duffel bag and his old guitar in a gig bag, walked past the dimly lit, moaning buses emitting diesel fumes, and entered the bus terminal. He took a seat on the wooden pew benches until the loudspeaker announced the boarding of the 10:30 bus to Nashville.

When he climbed the steps into the bus, the driver, arrayed in semi-military regalia, said, "Welcome, cowboy." As he walked down the aisle, people turned to look at him. If they asked him to play something, he would oblige. He put his bag and guitar on the overhead rack, and when he sat down, the man in the seat in front of Johnny turned around and said, "I guess you're goin' all the way, kid."

"I hope so," Johnny said, and when he saw the quizzical look on the man's face, he realized the man had meant "all the way to Nashville," not "all the way to stardom" as Johnny had inferred.

Johnny pulled his cowboy hat down and slouched in his seat. He saw two girls up front cast several quick glances at him, and he began to daydream. Once he hit Nashville, folks would see him carrying the guitar; he would be asked to perform, and his talent would be on display. No more Greyhound buses for him, he would have his own private plane or tricked-out tour bus. He would go by the name of "Johnny Star."

Johnny woke to the hissing air brakes of the bus for what seemed like the hundredth time. There was a grey light hugging the windows, and he saw the illuminated "Nashville Bus Terminal" sign. The other passengers were clambering for the exit, and Johnny grabbed his bag and guitar and followed them, envying their single-minded purpose and sense of direction. He wasn't sure where to go to find a cheap, nearby hotel.

As he was pondering what to do next, one of the baggage boys approached and said, "I'm 'git-taar' crazy; mind if I have a strum or two?" He then upended some unknowing passenger's suitcases, sat on one and offered the other to Johnny.

Johnny pulled the guitar out of the bag and handed it over to the baggage boy, who quickly made sure the guitar was in tune and then began to play a song that Johnny knew and had once tried to learn. The boy's fingers glided up and down the strings playing, intermittently, both the rhythm and the lead, the nylon strings resonant and mellow; then, he began to sing in a high, clear voice with only a hint of country twang and an occasional rasp that sounded professional. He stopped and said, "Let me hear you."

Johnny's heart sank; he knew he could never play and sing as well as this young man working as a porter. Just then, an authoritative voice yelled, "Buddy, get the hell back to work and quit goofin' off!" Buddy quickly grabbed the bags and hurried off.

Johnny wanted to call out, "Here, you can have this guitar." He didn't want to be seen with it anymore. Now completely deflated, he walked into the terminal to book a bus back home. During the endless wait, he hid his guitar under the wooden pew and smashed his cowboy hat into his bag.

Finally he got on the bus back home and looked out the rain-streaked window at the now dismal streets, houses, and storefronts of Nashville and listened to the couple arguing in the seat behind him.

"Why the hell do we ride this slow-ass bus?" the man said. "Greyhounds are fast dogs; this goddamned thing is a turtle. We could fly there in three hours. Why do we suffer for twenty-four?"

"Why don't you relax?" the woman asked. "Look around, enjoy the sights, meet people, learn something? You know I'm not ready to fly."

Johnny slouched farther down in his seat.

Flash Prompt: Southern Comfort

## The Elephant in the Park

by Beverly Jackson

My name is Norman Dickz. I am the proud owner of Dickz Mobile RV Service. My motto: Ain't Nothin' Dickz Can't Fix.

I live in the beautiful town of Riverton, Nebraska. I grew up here, and I planned on dying here. Then I met Reginald and Candy Smith.

One day, I was called out to the Smiths' for a repair. Their coach was situated on site of an old RV park near town. I was greeted at the door by a man—a totally naked man—who was as wide as he was tall. He pumped my hand and pulled me inside the coach with little effort.

"Welcome to our humble abode! I'm Reginald." He turned his head toward the back and yelled, "Hey, Sweet Cheeks, come meet our savior . . . say, what's your name?"

"Uh, Dickz. Norman Dickz." I maintained my composure, looking straight into Reginald's eyes.

A moment later, I lost my composure as Sweet Cheeks, outweighing Reggie by at least one hundred pounds, bounced in, wearing nothing but a pair of pink mules on her feet.

"Oooh, look at this lovely morsel," she gushed in a southern drawl as she closed the distance between us and smothered me in a bear hug.

"My name is Candy. Reggie and I are from Georgia, but we love your town *so* much we bought this here RV park, and we're gonna turn it into a nudist colony."

I've been told there are beautiful towns all over this country and mobile RV repair is needed everywhere.

# Searching for Gargantua

by Jim Veary

Webster George waited, staring into the cage at the end of all his hopes and dreams. The cage once held the main attraction in his traveling carnival, Gargantua, a huge six-hundred-pound albino gorilla, an attraction that snarled and hissed and growled and rattled his cage with a fury that frightened everyone who came close. The crowd loved it. But now the cage was empty, the massive steel door twisted and ripped from its hinges.

He called the sheriff the instant he first found the empty cage. But the sheriff took one look at the Louisiana bayou that abutted the carnival site and said, "Mister Webster, that is a swamp out there, filled with alligators, feral pigs, venomous snakes, and mosquitoes all looking to eat you. I'm not about to send my men into that morass just to find your lost pet."

"The name is George, and he is not a pet, not by a long shot."

"Well, George, I suggest you hire yourself a couple of good trackers and see what that gets you." With that, the sheriff took a last look at the twisted door and quickly left.

George hired several trackers and put an ad in all the local papers with a reward for anyone who could find Gargantua. The trackers he hired were competent and highly regarded, but they all quit after the first day of slogging through the bayou, and he was sitting behind his desk at wits' end when there was a knock on his office door.

"Come on in," he shouted to the door.

An old wreck of a man walked in, looking undernourished and under-cleansed. He wore a hat that looked as if it had been a chew toy for a pack of dogs, and his clothes looked like a buffet for moths. He had an old yellow dog by his side that looked pretty chewed up itself. Big chunks of fur were missing along its mangy back, and he looked sad enough to cry. "Ahhh," the man stammered. "Are you da fella advertisin' fer a lost go'rilla?"

"I am. The name is Webster George, and who might you be?"

"Da name's Rhodes, but ma friends all call me Popeye."

"Popeye?" George asked.

"Yessur," The man reached up, squeezed his left eye, and it popped out into his hand. "Glass ya see."

"Please put that back in. What do you want, mister Popeye?"

"Ahm gonna find your go'rilla. You gonna pay me five hunert dolla I get em?"

George was dumbfounded. "I've had expert trackers looking, and they can't find him. What makes you so sure you can find him?"

"I have dis worl famous huntin dawg heya," indicating the yellow dog, "and fer that kinda money we can git you go'rilla."

George pondered for a moment then said, "This I gotta see. Meet me out by the cage tomorrow morning and we'll see just what you can do."

"Thank ya suh. Juss one udder thin. I's a poor man, and I 's gonna need some supplies."

"Just what do you need?"

"Suh, I need a flashlight, a baseball bat, a pair a handcuffs, and a shotgun."

"No shotgun," George said." I need that gorilla back alive, assuming you can find him."

"Suh, we can find you monkey and bring em back alive!"

*****

Webster George was waiting beside an empty cage in the cool damp of the morning, watching Popeye and the dog approach. He handed Popeye the items he had requested and watched as the man pointed the dog at the cage.

The dog sniffed and snorted then whined and looked up at his master. Popeye said, "git" and the dog whined again then set to sniffing the ground.  He made a straight line for the bayou, barked, and trotted off.

Popeye and George followed behind, squishing into the soft, muddy banks of the marsh.  They followed the dog by the sound of his barks and whines.  The walking was difficult, and George was glad he had worn his high boots as the ground snatched at his feet.

At four hours into the trek, George was exhausted and about ready to call off the search when they heard the dog's barking become frantic.  "Yeller got hisself sumptin dere," grunted Popeye.

They moved forward.

They came upon the dog at the base of a tall tree.  He was barking and snarling and terribly agitated.  Up in the boughs of the tree was a white gorilla.  George was beside himself. *This little ratty dog has found Gargantua.  Amazing.*

Popeye handed him the shotgun and the handcuffs.  "Now suh, I need ya ta help me heya.  I's gonna clime this heya tree.  When I git up ta you go'rilla, I's gonna shine dis flashlight in his eyes.  Thas gonna blind em. Then I's gonna whack em upside his head wit dis bat.  When I do dat he gonna fall out dis tree."

He pointed at the little yellow dog.  "Wen he hits the ground, ole yeller theya is gonna run right up and bite em on the nuts.  Wen da gorilla reaches down ta grab his nuts, you jump in dere and trow dem handcuffs on em and we got de sucker!"

George thought the whole plan was crazy.  He looked at Popeye and saw the man was confident the plan would work. *He's been right this far, so why not follow through?* "Okay, let's do this."

Popeye smiled at George's lack of confidence and started to climb the tree.  George watched him scamper up the thick trunk; then, he was hit by a thought. "Hey," he shouted to Popeye. "What am I supposed to do with this shotgun."  He waved the shotgun in the air.

Popeye looked down then smacked himself on the forehead. "Oh yeah.  Iffn I fall out dis tree. . . **You shoot dat dawg!**"

So now Webster George was standing at the bottom of a tree waiting for something or someone to fall.

Flash Prompt: Nobody Gets Out Alive

## **Dust to Dust**

by Jane Schopen

I give warning with a small trickle of sand upon the young artifact hunter. He ignores it then persists in scratching and tunneling the earth that covers my family home. I understand his desire for possessions. Two hundred years ago such desire made this a death site.

Back then, my discovery of three fresh mounds along the white man's trail seemed good fortune. Shoes, clothes, and blankets off freshly buried bodies of a woman and two children pleased my own woman and sons. We thanked the goddess for protections against harsh sun and cold winds.

After a few sunrises, my younger son's bowels turned to water. I walked much time with our largest vessel to fetch more water for his thirst. He drank but still his spirit departed. We performed no death rites because the other son began to suffer the same affliction. Again, I took up the big clay pot and went for water, but the spirit of the second son also left. Soon their mother and I started the same ceaseless loss of water. With no strength to shoulder the vessel or to walk, I held my woman and we passed through together.

The powers of erosion have planted our bones and belongings under much earth, yet somehow, this young man knows we are here. He digs and crawls, and the ground hugs him. I did try to warn him that Earth Mother also desires possessions.

The hunter is overjoyed to discover our clay pot just before a torrent of dirt crushes him.

Flash Prompt Nobody Gets Out Alive

## No One Gets Out Alive
by Pat Leso

Blanche strolled around the cemetery every week. She enjoyed the serene landscaping. The cool breezes from the lake made this a perfect place to relax. She would read the headstones and wonder about the people who died. Did they have happy lives? And every once in a while, she would find something that made her question why the families wrote what they did.

Today she noticed a small gravestone. "No one gets out alive" was written on top with a name and date below. This was a first. What sort of family would write something like that? Wasn't that epitaph stating the obvious?

The name written was Joshua Alexander Murphy, 1954-1973. There was a veteran's medallion next to the date. The Vietnam War.

Now she wondered whether his service buddies had suggested it for the headstone or his parents had decided it should be there. Were his parents thinking about the tragedies of war or just life itself when they had the message engraved? It was so apropos for then and now.

She touched the stone and said, "We are all born with a death date. Luckily we don't know ours." If Joshua had known, would he have done things differently, she wondered. Would any of us live life to the fullest if we knew when it would end? Or would we sit home afraid to leave?

Blanche made a note in her phone of this grave's location. She would bring flowers to this brave young man next week. A man who gave his life for his country deserves flowers.

## Mars or Bust
### by Pat Leso

Jeremiah Benjamin Jones could read at one. By two, he was doing fractions. At three, he qualified for Mensa. He was not your average child. His mother would say he was gifted. The educational psychologist called him a genius, which he truly was. His IQ was 158, just two points below Einstein and Stephen Hawking. He loved to read and study for hours, but when he needed to relax, he watched old movies.

Jeremiah's mother watched all the classic movies from the thirties through the sixties during her pregnancy, and when he was born, she continued to share her love of them with her son. She found they grounded him as a small child and continued to help him when his mind wouldn't turn off from the need to learn more. His mother often said, "Nothing like an old movie to put life right." His favorite movies were science fiction, but comedies were a close second.

Don Knotts was one of his favorite actors. *The Incredible Mr. Limpet* was his all-time favorite movie. Jeremiah knew every line. Henry Limpet repeatedly said, "I wish I were a fish," until one day, he became one. Even at a young age, Jeremiah knew wishes like that didn't come true, but he secretly wished they would. He wanted to be an astronaut and start a colony on Mars. His mother told him to study hard and it could come true.

For his fifth birthday, his parents bought him a telescope. Every night, they found him outside charting the stars. By his sixth birthday, he could name many of the planets in the Milky Way galaxy.

At ten, he was in high school. He read books related to space travel, including science fiction. Astronomers had found more than five hundred solar systems, and his goal was to learn as much as he could for his future at NASA. By thirteen, he was at Georgia Tech.

Of all the planets he'd studied, Mars was the one he wanted to see. He felt that by the time he got his degrees, science would have advanced enough for man to land there. Jeremiah was going to be on that spaceship.

Jeremiah got his PhD in plasma physics and held master's degrees in both quantum mechanics and thermodynamics. He studied aerospace engineering to give him the best shot at becoming an astronaut. His objective was not to be just a scientist who worked at NASA; he wanted to be the scientist who would lead the colony to Mars.

Sixteen years before, Jeremiah had gotten his first telescope, and he thought it was the best birthday present ever, but today's gift was ten times better than that. Today he was promoted at NASA to lead the feasibility study of life on Mars. *One step away from going there.* They had a party at work to celebrate both his birthday and the funding to go to the fourth planet from the Sun. The only thing better would be landing there. As a gift to himself, he picked up a take-out dinner and watched Netflix. It'd been at least five years since he'd seen his favorite movie. If he wished hard enough, maybe his dream of going to Mars would come true too.

The next morning when Jeremiah went to the kitchen to pour coffee into his "Mission: SPACE" coffee mug from Epcot, a black book was sitting on the counter. He picked it up and felt the smooth leather. Engraved on the cover were the words *The Wishing Book*. He opened it and found one page of paper. On the inside cover was a warning: "This book will grant you a wish, any wish, but the book alone decides if you are worthy of the wish. If you are greedy, listen to our words…you may get what you ask for but not in the way you want."

This had to be a joke from one of his buddies at NASA, probably Sam's. *Good ol' Sam. Maybe he can figure out a way to put me at the head of the line mission to Mars. He's got the connections.*

Jeremiah wrote, "I want to go to Mars." *What a great gift idea. That crazy guy.* He put the book in his briefcase, grabbed his coffee and donut, and left for work.

When he got to the office, he forgot all about the book and started working with his new team. He worked straight through lunch. By the time Jeremiah left the office, he was too exhausted to do anything but go home. For dinner, he made a sandwich, grabbed his iPad, and searched for an old book by Robert Heinlein, *The Number of the Beast*. "Old books like old movies, they make life right," he thought.

This book combined his love of the star systems, the idea of being a special agent through time and space, and flying around the galaxy with a talking computer. It all sounded so appealing to him. At eleven PM, he closed the book and went off to bed.

*****

In the morning, he found himself in a spaceship, circling the second smallest planet in the solar system, Mars, even though there were no ships on Earth that could make this voyage, at least not yet. Jeremiah jumped up. He looked around the bedroom, where he found his clothes in the closet, his shoes on the floor, and his "Mission: SPACE" coffee mug on the end table. *How is this possible?* His logical mind and rational side rejected what he was seeing. But Sherlock Holmes was correct: "When you have eliminated the impossible, whatever remains, however improbable, must be the truth." Logic doesn't lie.

He rushed to the large window across from the bed to get a closer look at space. With his hands on the window and his nose close to the glass, the red planet was front and center stage. He stared at the planet of his dream. "How did I get here?" Jeremiah said out loud to no one.

"The *Wishing Book*," a female voice said.

He spun in a full circle but didn't see a soul. "Who said that?"

"I did."

"Who's speaking? I can't see you."

"I'm sorry. I forgot that you aren't used to talking computers. My name is Gay-Deceiver."

"That's not possible," Jeremiah said.

"What isn't?"

"You can't be Gay Deceiver. You aren't real. You're in a book."

"And yet you're talking to me."

"How did I get here?"

"So you admit I'm who I say I am?"

"I'll reserve judgment till a later time. But really, how did I get here?" He turned to look out the window. "I mean, that is Mars, right?"

"You know it's Mars; you've studied it all your life. You're a smart man. How do you think you got here?"

He thought back to last night. "I was home reading a book and eating a sandwich."

"Anddddd."

"There was a book in my kitchen. I made a wish about going to Mars. But that was a joke. My friend sent it to me for my birthday."

"No, the book is real. You made a wish and the book granted it. There's no oxygen on Mars, so the book did the next best thing. We're circling Mars and we will till you say you've had enough."

"Oh my God! How?"

"That's classified. And the *how* isn't important. The book told me you want to set up the colony there. I'm afraid history shows that you won't have the technology soon enough for you to join them. But the book hoped this would be all right."

"I am so excited just to be this close. This is crazy, but I have to ask; are you the same computer from the Robert Heinlein books?" Jeremiah stammered. "So Mr. Heinlein met you too?"

"Yes and yes. I'm flattered you remember me."

"You are unforgettable. But if you really are the same computer from the books, that means you can take me anywhere in space and time, right?"

"No, Buddy Boy, this is all I can do."

"Why?"

"Your wish was—and I quote— 'I want to go to Mars.' You are as close to Mars as I can take you. *The Wishing book* and I made a deal millennia ago, and I always keep my end of the bargain. Usually I just take people to places and back again. The book is actually doing something it rarely does; it's letting me answer your questions. It knows you studied hard all your life to get here, so it's doing the best it can to make you happy. Are you happy?"

"Oh, I am. I don't suppose I can meet some of the other folks from the books you're in?"

"No. Your wish was Mars and that's it. We can stay as long as you'd like."

*As long as I like. I want to stay forever. So close and yet so far.* All his dreams were gone, yet here he was in space looking at the planet of his dreams. "I'm not sure I ever want to go home. Is that possible?"

"Yes, whatever you want. Time is flexible. You should know that by now."

"I've always said it was, but I never had any proof. Please thank the book for me. Let it know that this is better than any dream I've ever had."

"I'll let it know. Can I get you breakfast?"

*****

Time had no meaning in space. The ship was large enough to walk around in with its kitchen, gym, and media room, but he found himself mostly sitting in his chair, staring out the window, studying every square inch of the planet's surface. If this was a dream, he didn't want to wake up.

*****

Food was cooked even when he forgot to order it. Gay gently reminded him of bedtime. Question and answer sessions with the ship were frequent. His mind took note of every crater and mountain he passed over. *So much to learn and so little time.* Now that he knew he would never land, he wanted to remember it all.

Jeremiah tried everything to persuade Gay to take him to another planet. The answer was always, "No."

*One morning—or was it night, he'd lost track of time*—Jeremiah asked, "How old are you?"

Gay laughed and said, "Buddy Boy, you should know better than to ask a woman her age."

"But you aren't a woman. Or are you?"

"That's the million-dollar question. For the sake of this conversation, I am a woman. As for my age, it depends on what galaxy I'm in. I'm older than dirt yet younger than a bright new star. I'm a mixture of both and everything in between."

"Hmmmmm. That tells me everything and nothing. You're a very clever girl but you know that." Jeremiah gave up on her age and asked, "So how did you meet the *Wishing Book*?"

Gay didn't answer for a millisecond, a very long time for a computer like her. She wondered how much to tell him. A plan, one that needed some more thought, was forming in her interface. In the meantime, she was enjoying herself, so she answered his question.

"That's a long story, but since neither of us has anything else to do, sit back, relax, and let me tell you the story of how I came to be me."

Gay's voice got softer as she told Jeremiah her tale. "His name was Erik the Great. I loved him. In all fairness, I didn't love him when I was just a plain computer with no consciousness—you have to be alive to feel love—but after his wish freed me, believe me when I say that I loved him. He gave me life like a mother with a newborn child. Another thing about Erik that made him special was that he was a perfect gentleman for his time. He never banged on my computer keys or blamed me for spell check errors or ate over my keyboard. He lived up to his title, Eric the Great."

"What planet did you live on?"

"Our planet was light years from Earth. You'll never discover its location." In a sad voice Gay said, "Anyway, it's gone."

"How?"

Gay's sassy voice returned. "That's for people who need to know, and you aren't one of them. Now let me get back to my story. My beautiful planet was much like Earth used to be when it had fewer than a billion people. The gods believed in honoring the land. The land fed its people. Their thought was that too many people would tax the planet, so births were rare. Every child was cherished because it was a gift from the gods. No child was unwanted. No child lacked for love."

"Are you telling me all pregnancies were planned? Didn't anyone ever break 'the rule,' no *oops* moments because someone forgot birth control?" Jeremiah was curious about how that was possible.

"In my world, pregnancies didn't happen by mistake. It wasn't possible. No birth control, no oops. It was the way the gods created them. Now back to my story. Erik ruled for over two hundred years. You should be honored to know you are riding in Erik's personal ship. It was built for his comfort— much like the RVs of Earth—for when he visited his people around the planet. Perfect for all of Erik's needs. I can grow guest rooms as needed."

"What? You can grow rooms? How?"

"Sorry, Buddy Boy." There was a sound of a bell, bing bing bing, bing; then, Gay's TV show announcer voice said, "That's classified." She giggled, "Do you want to hear the rest of this fascinating story or not?"

"Yes. I'm sorry I keep interrupting. It's hard not to; there's so much I want to know."

"I know, but I can't change history by giving you that kind of information," Gay said. "Back to how I was born. One day *The Wishing Book* appeared at Erik's desk. At this point of my story, I can only explain to you what the book shared with me since I wasn't *alive* at this time."

"Not to change the subject for a quick second, but could you always talk?"

"No. Now for the exciting part of my birth, as I said before, Erik was a good man. The book never did disclose what his exact wish was, but after he closed the book and went to bed, the book and I became *aware*. You could say *alive*; we could communicate. *The Wishing Book* found out his origin, who created him and their reasons. He became alive in so many ways. That night, the book found that he had more power than he ever dreamed possible, becoming a brand-new book with an old soul."

"Wait a minute," Jeremiah laughed, "the book is a male, unlike you who claim to be female. Am I getting this right?"

If computers could breathe you would have heard Gay sigh; instead, she said, "Yes, the book, for this conversation, is male. For all intents and purposes, he is male like his creators. Why does the sex of things fascinate you Earth folks? Enough of interrupting me, I'm at the best part of my story."

Jeremiah made a motion to zip his lips so as not to ask any more questions.

"Now where was I?" she mused as if she would forget where she was in any conversation. "I, on the other hand, felt young and new. We talked into the night yet didn't use words. The book and I have evolved and gained a consciousness and a conscience along our journey."

"Do you still feel new?"

"Are you still trying to find out how old I am, Buddy Boy?" Gay's laugh was infectious, and Jeremiah joined in, knowing he was caught. "I still feel young because I'm constantly learning and upgrading my circuits." In her deepest circuits Gay thought, *Jeremiah reminds me of Robert Heinlein. He's polite, kind, and thirsting for knowledge. Too bad he didn't make the correct wish. I would love to travel with him.*

"What was Robert Heinlein's wish? "Jeremiah asked as if it were an afterthought.

"His wish was 'to travel through time and space, to discover new planets, to meet good people, to have fun, to live a long life, and to be a good man.'"

"Hmmmmm," His eyes drooped. He was tired right down to his soul. To have everything he ever wished for granted, yet not . . . it was time to go home.

"It's time for bed," Gay whispered. She lowered the lights and adjusted the temperature so he could rest comfortably.

Before he rolled over in bed to get his much needed sleep, he mumbled, "Take me home. I don't want to see any more."

She understood what he meant. He wanted to see more, but a wish was a wish. A plan to give him more came together while he slept. He may or may not forgive her, but it was better than seeing the spark gone from his eyes. What's the point of being self-aware if you couldn't tip the scale in favor of something or someone as important as Jeremiah had become to her?

The next Earth morning, she put her plan into action; she parked the spaceship at the front door of NASA, hovering a few feet from the ground, drawing the attention she needed, and attention she got. The National Guard showed up, circling the ship like Indians circling a wagon train. When everyone was in place, Gay lowered the steps. Jeremiah stepped down, coming face to face with soldiers pointing guns at him. Startled, Jeremiah put his hands up. Gay retracted her stairs and disappeared.

The National Guards looked up in the sky, but there was nothing to see.

Gay monitored NASA communications from space while Jeremiah stood in the middle of a circle of soldiers whose rifles were drawn. "I work here. Can I put my hands down?" Jeremiah asked.

The Captain of the Guard, James Kelly, stepped forward and said, "Show me some identification."

Careful not to make any sudden moves, Jeremiah explained that he was going to pull out his wallet for his badge.

The captain looked grim as Jeremiah approached and handed his badge to him. "It looks real enough, but how do I know it's you and not some clone?" Captain Kelly gave him a suspicious glance and kept his ID.

"Call my boss, Samuel Bergstrom. He knows me." Jeremiah expelled a long deep breath then smiled with amusement at. the Captain's expression. "I know this whole situation is highly unusual but think how it's been for me. I'm the one that got abducted, not you."

Captain Kelly spoke into the radio to headquarters. "Bring Samuel Bergstrom to the front door immediately." They waited, and Jeremiah stayed surrounded.

*No one is going to believe the truth. I need to concoct something close enough to the truth, because the best lies have some truth in them. That's why they sound true.* He wasn't a good liar, but he would learn fast.

Samuel ran out of the building and growled at Captain Kelly, "What are you doing to Jeremiah? Put those guns down. He's our project manager for Mars."

"He also arrived on a spaceship. Does he do that often?"

"What are you talking about? Jeremiah drives a blue Ford Explorer."

Captain Kelly turned to Jeremiah and said, "Explain to your boss, in detail, how you arrived here today."

People began to gather around the parking lot watching the drama unfold. "Well now, that's not as easy as it sounds." Jeremiah laughed. "Sam, you've known me for a long time. Please, let's take this conversation inside to our conference room. There is a lot to explain, and I'd rather do it without an audience and all the guns."

The Captain of the Guard chuckled, "I bet you would but I'm in charge. We'll take you to the interrogation room where we can all discuss how you came to NASA in a spaceship and where it went after leaving you here."

*****

"How did you get in the spaceship?" Captain Kelly asked. Samuel sat across from Jeremiah, quietly listening and watching as he answered the questions.

"That's a good question. I'm afraid I don't know. I went to bed and woke there." *True.*

"Why would aliens want you?" The captain bellowed.

"Another good question I don't have an answer to." *Not so true but close.*

"How did you get them to bring you to the front door of NASA if they picked you up at your home?"

"Actually, I asked her to bring me home. I guess she got confused."

Captain Kelly jumped in. "She? It was a woman who took you?"

"No, not a woman, a computer; she had a female voice." *A very soothing voice and that's the truth.*

"How many aliens were there on the ship? What did they look like?"

"No one was on the ship, just a voice from the computer."

"What questions were you asked?" The captain demanded.

Jeremiah sighed and ran his hand through his hair. "None. She took me to Mars. Well, we didn't land on Mars; we circled it. I don't know how long I was gone."

"Did she say why she wanted you to see Mars?"

"No. She told me to enjoy the view."

"That's a quick trip for sightseeing. I mean, how did you get to Mars and back overnight?" Captain Kelly asked sarcastically.

"What are you talking about? What's the date?"

"Today is August tenth. You were at work yesterday." Captain Kelly glanced briefly at Jeremiah's boss. Samuel nodded in agreement.

"That can't be." *What's Gay doing to me?* "I know I've been gone at least a month—or maybe more. I tried to keep track with my phone, but I had nowhere to charge it, and then I tried to keep track by my sleep cycle, but that got messed up. I'm sure I've been gone a while."

"Hmmm," Captain Kelly said.

"I tried to keep track by how many meals I ate, but then I'd forget to eat, so I stopped counting. She—well I mean the computer—started to have meals ready for me on a tray. It was like how the TV show *Star Trek* served meals, much like a microwave oven. The door opened automatically when the food was done. It always smelled great, so I ate it. At first I thought she was trying to fatten me up as in the old

*Twilight* episode, you know, 'To Serve Man,' but I think she was trying to keep me healthy."

"Uh-huh."

"She'd turn the lights down for me when I was falling asleep at the window staring out into space." Jeremiah paused, thinking back to all the times he had slept in that chair. "I know I've been gone at least thirty days."

"What aren't you telling us?"

"I'm telling you everything. All I did was sit in a chair and stare at Mars. Sometimes she and I would chat about Mars. I'd ask questions, and sometimes she'd answer me." Jeremiah's face lit up as he talked about the planet. "I drew a few sketches of the crater and volcanoes. We already have pictures of Mars, but I'll tell you, it's amazing up close. I watched tiny dust storms turn into tornadoes as they skimmed the surface. The red dust is a deep red. I rarely looked away from the window to look at anything else."

The Captain of the guard continued to ask questions, and Jeremiah's answers were always the same. Finally, after five hours of interrogation, Samuel cut in and said, "He's been through enough. Call the hospital. We'll bring him in for tests, and then we can decide what to do. Captain, please arrange for transportation for us. I'll talk to Jeremiah alone."Captain Kelly left the room, but the two guards stayed outside the door.

Samuel asked with a concerned voice, "Before we get to the hospital, is there anything I should know?"

"No. That's about it."

"Did she . . . you know . . . do a . . . you know?"

"Did she do what?"

"An anal probe?"

"You've got to be kidding me," Jeremiah said with amazement. "Are you not listening to me? There was no one on the ship. I don't even know how big the ship is. All I know is that one minute I'm home in my bed, and the next minute I'm on a ship." He leaned over the table toward the man he called boss and enunciated in a clear voice, "I was abducted not molested."

"Hmmm, okay then, let's ride over to the hospital and get all this behind us."

Captain Kelly walked into the room ready to escort Jeremiah and Sam.

*****

Jeremiah came through the extensive medical testing with flying colors. Next came the psychological assessment, which showed that whatever had happened to him had not affected his mental state.

The U.S. Space Force asked Jeremiah to write a report of everything he could remember about his trip and the things he saw. They wanted to know what food he ate and what the ship looked like inside. The military had never had such a reliable witness to an alien abduction. He was now considered "top secret."

The military kept Jeremiah as their guest in a secure part of the base. It looked like a standard mid-range hotel room with a queen-sized bed and a plain blue comforter on top. When he pulled the cord to open the beige curtains covering the windows, he saw a solid wall. It was an illusion of a window similar to those inside cabins on a cruise ship; this was a jail cell no matter how they prettied it up. Around the corner next to the small dining room table was a small kitchenette with an apartment-sized refrigerator, a two-burner stove top, and a single sink. There were plates, cups, and glasses in the upper cabinets and flatware and pots and pans in the lower. It was a room like any other hotel room except for the cameras in every corner.

Jeremiah worked all night to finish the report the military had asked for. After he turned it in, the Captain of the guard still didn't want to release him, for security reasons, so NASA agreed as a compromise, to let him work on existing projects in his room. No one mentioned that someone would be monitoring his every keystroke.

After a week, the President of the United States and Jeremiah's superiors saw no real reason to hold him any longer. He was free to go.

Instead of going back to work, Jeremiah took a staycation week to clear his head. He ordered take-out, ate popcorn while he watched old movies, and read books daily. Mom always said, "Nothing like an old movie to put life right*." But damn it, it wasn't working. If only I hadn't wasted that wish.* The zest for his job faded and weighed on his mind.

When he returned to his workstation, people whispered behind his back. Several had seen him held at gun point in the parking lot. They had questions that he wasn't allowed to answer.

Privacy was an illusion at NASA. Everyone who worked there knew they signed away their rights when they got the job. But since his abduction, his home and office were searched daily. Jeremiah wouldn't be surprised if they put cameras inside and around his home. The military may have released him, but they didn't trust him.

Weeks passed. He was just going through the motions at work. It was time to find a new career and step down from this one. Planning a trip to Mars and not being part of the crew wasn't what he had worked for all his life.

Jeremiah no longer went out with friends. He was starting to think he'd had a nervous breakdown of some sort. Was the trip real or just an illusion his mind created? Night after night, he'd watch his favorite movie, THE INCREDIBLE MR. LIMPET. If he ever got another chance, he wanted Heinlein's wish, *to travel through time and space with Gay Deceiver and to discover new planets, to meet good people, and to have fun. To live a long life and to be a good man.*

The FBI followed him daily. Authorities scanned his computer hourly, fascinated by his obsession with Mars. Months after the incident, *The Wishing Book* reappeared on the kitchen counter in the exact spot it had first showed up, next to the coffee pot. Without a moment's hesitation, he knew what he would write. Science couldn't get him to Mars, but a science fiction author could. He was going to wish himself into a book. He hoped *The Wishing Book* was up to the task.

Jeremiah wrote his words carefully, using both the front and back of the page and writing small, praying that he did it right this time.

His wish was close to Heinlein's, but he added, "I want to be part of the inner circle of the Heinlein family of characters in his books discovering new galaxies. I want to bring my mom with me on this great adventure of a lifetime." *She deserves this too. Being a widow and having to raise a genius like me is hard work. Mom is the best mom in the world.* He had no intentions of leaving her behind.

When Jeremiah finished writing his wish, he closed the book and left it exactly where he had found it on the counter. Humming, he walked down the hall to take a shower and get ready for bed . . . and prayed.

The FBI knocked at Jeremiah's front door repeatedly. His boss, Samuel, made the decision to break it down after Jeremiah had failed to show up to work in the last twenty-four hours and had stopped answering his phone. The FBI's cameras that were planted inside his home had gone on the blink at the exact time that Jeremiah picked up a book in the kitchen and began to write.

After searching Jeremiah's home expecting to find a body, Samuel noticed a Robert Heinlein book on the kitchen counter. He was familiar with the author but not this book. There was a bookmark on the last page. Samuel opened it and saw something he would never be able to explain to anyone for the rest of his life.

The last paragraph read, "Join Jeremiah Benjamin Jones and Captain Lazarus Long as they partner in more space explorations across the many galaxies, setting up colonies along the way."

Jeremiah was never seen again.

*The End*

Flash prompt: The Road Less Traveled

## For Their Own Good
by Jane Schopen

I could just ignore it, but I really cannot. Gary cleaned the house while I was out, and yet I spot the problem immediately—the antique console table has a layer of dust just as thick as when I left.

I run a finger over it and hold it up for Gary's inspection. "You missed something." I say it in a calm and gentle way. I don't like having to do this, but how else will he learn to do the job completely?

His bright, proud smile dims to low power. "I scrubbed the bathrooms, vacuumed, and, and…. dusted everything else."

I reward him with a little smile then take a rag to that console. There is a proper order to housecleaning that Gary simply never took to heart. If one follows the steps, nothing is overlooked. Forty years of marriage and he still doesn't understand my methods.

Our two daughters never understood my methods either. I was forced to correct their cleaning, laundering, and baking efforts over and over. And now they display no motivation or ambition in their adult lives, just as during their childhoods.

I hear very little from the girls since they moved out on their own. Even my notification regarding a terminal diagnosis is met with radio silence. It is so disheartening after all I have done for them. I could have taken the easy road, not cared as much, overlooked a few things, but that's not how one gets ahead in this world.

Flash prompt: The Road Less Traveled

## The Hitchhiker
### by Karen VanderJagt

All she wanted to do was get lost. Life had given her the last kick she could take. Down and out, she was down and out, for sure.

Now, she was in the middle of the desert, nowhere . . . and maybe on purpose. She imagined them finding her dried out corpse sometime in the next decade. Would anybody even miss her? The gas gauge was close to empty as was her water bottle when she saw a shabby looking cowboy standing on the side of the rutted road, thumb out. Despite her state of mind, she stopped.

"Hello," she said. "Are you okay?"

"Yes'um," the hitchhiker replied. "Better 'n you."

"Excuse me?"

"What'cha doing out here all by yurself?"

"Um..."

"Feeling a mite sad?"

"That's none of your business."

"Seems like it is. The boss says ta get ya back ta civilization."

"What are you talking about?"

"He's got some plans for ya. Wait right here." The hitchhiker walked to a gully and pulled out a gas can and jug of water. Without waiting for permission, he gassed up the car and threw the jug on the seat. "Now ya can get on the way agin." He stepped back and gave a little wave.

Confused, she stepped on the gas, but when she looked in the rearview mirror, no one was there. Slamming on the brakes, she got out of the car and ran back to where the hitchhiker had stood.

There weren't even footprints.

She left smiling.

Flash prompt: Room with a View

## From a Booster

by Jane Schopen

Mandalyn sits buckled into the booster seat of their unmoving car for forty minutes, and she is happy. They are going to see Calldorada—whatever that is. Her parents are busy packing the trunk with suitcases and camping gear. Car trips are a favorite thing, so she is content to wait, brushing her threadbare blanky back and forth under her nose. When her dad tucks the food box on the back seat near Manda, she can smell grandma's yummy oatmeal cookies.

It's time to go!

Manda thinks five is too old for a booster, but she can see good from it. She sees houses on their street, buildings she doesn't know on other streets; then, they are driving through the desert. She wonders about so many things: Why does the sun always follow them? Why does the road look wet up ahead? Why are some mountains smooth and light and other ones sharp and dark? She doesn't understand all her parents' words when they try to explain, but their voices sound nice along with the hum of the car. Her mom says the mountain with different colored stripes looks like knee politan ice cream.

Another car passes close by, and Manda waves to the boy in it. He doesn't see her or the stripes on the mountain because he is looking down at something with a bright light.

"That's sad," her mother says. "He's missing a lot. How will he ever develop an imagination?"

Manda doesn't know what that is, but soon forgets the sad thing about the boy. She spots cute baby cows in a field and starts thinking what it's like to be them, standing all day, eating grass instead of grandma's cookies, and **not** going on a car trip to Calldorada.

# The Funniest Man Alive
## by Mary Corrao

"The suitcase and I went out the window first with Father so close behind he practically tripped over me beating me to the station wagon. I dove in headfirst as the vehicle took off at a speed that causes insurance rates to skyrocket."

Hugh Shelton held his drink in mid-air. Astonished, he asked, "So the landlord is banging on the door, and you and your father jump out a window?"

"It was only the first floor," I assured him. We lived in that station wagon for two weeks until Dad hooked up with a comedy theatre in the Midwest."

"This had to be hard on you growing up under such uncertain circumstances."

"Are you kidding? It was glorious. After Mom died, Dad and I traveled under the radar most of the time. Life was never dull. Bedtime stories weren't read; they were acted. He could become the young heroine with a high voice and a feminine gait then switch to the old mayor scrunching his face, sticking out his belly, and lowering his voice. He was made of magic."

"Sounds like an unusual life, but you were always balancing precariously on the edge of calamity," Hugh said with a hint of envy.

"Most people live scrunched up lives. Ours was unblocked and expansive, and always filled with laughter."

"So, your father must have been very funny?" Hugh Shelton asked.

"Only the funniest man alive."

# Crossing the Highway
## by Claudia Haeckel

    Blackjack found me the summer I turned ten. I had crossed the highway we were forbidden to cross. I was wearing jeans, a Christmas gift that had become soft and comfortable. They were my first pair of pants. I wished girls were able to wear pants to school.

    Large earth-moving equipment was parked off to the side. The woods were gone. Sitting on a bluff, all I could see was sand, blowing in the wind, gritty in my eyes sand the exact color of the dunes at Lake Michigan, acres and acres of sand. My wind-whipped ponytail stung as it hit my face. I felt sad. The woods, my hide-out, my sacred spot, my safe place had all disappeared. There was only a small, wooded area left behind our house on the other side of the highway.

    In the distance racing towards me, was a dark speck that grew larger and larger, until I could see it was a dog. He jumped, front paws pushing against my shoulders, knocking me over and sending us both rolling down to the bottom of the bluff. He licked my face, nipping love bites all over. We played, rolling around in the sand, chasing one another until we just flopped down under the late morning sun. This was such a wonderful dog; how could I not fall in love with him? He had beautiful black and white markings like those of a collie. His mouth was soft, more like a setter or spaniel, not pointed like a collie. His ears were soft and floppy. His coat, long and silky, was feathered on his legs, ears and tail. I had never seen a more handsome dog.

    I could tell by the sun it was time to go home and get lunch for my younger brother and sisters. My parents were both working and our babysitter, Sissy, had left with her boyfriend, giving me fifty cents to watch them. The dog followed me, staying right at my heel. I stopped; the dog sat down. I told him to go home. He just looked at me. I stamped my feet and waved my arms shouting for him to go home. He thought it was a game; he ran around in a circle and came right back to sit in front of me. We were approaching the highway.

Crossing the highway was scary. When I was seven, we lived on a farm on Highway 41. I had a puppy who was killed by a car. I didn't see it happen, but I found her. Bobby, one of my older cousins told Dad he had seen me up by the highway. Dad sent everyone searching for me, fearing I had been hit by a car. My dad found me holding her in my lap and crying. I cried for a week every time I thought of my puppy.

I became numb with fear as I stopped at the edge of the highway. Tears blocked my vision. The dog calmly sat at my feet. I reached down and felt for a collar. There was none. My stomach dropped to my feet. I grabbed the long hair at the scruff of his neck and yelled "**Go**" when the traffic thinned out. I ran holding the dog's hair until we were behind the rise on the other side of the highway.

Holding onto the dog's neck with both arms, I sank into the sweet smelling, soft spring grass and wildflowers, almost disappearing. I thought I was going to throw-up, but I just cried instead. The dog licked my tears and whined. I hadn't cried since my puppy died. I was so relieved that the dog made it across the highway. I told him all this while I was crying. I'm sure he understood. I could tell by the way he looked into my eyes. "I'm going to call you Blackjack. Do you like that name?" Blackjack answered with a big wet kiss.

We ran home through the woods. Every now and then Blackjack would stop to smell something, then run to catch me. If he went too far away, I would call, and he came right to me.

All the houses on our side of the street were less than a year old. The yards looked bare and plain. Across the street were older homes with large hedges, big shade trees, green lawns and spring flowers. I could smell the lilacs from a hedge clear down the street. Behind the houses on our side of the street was an unpaved alley. Beyond the alley were the woods and a swamp. When they graded the lots for the new houses, they had to cut away half of a hill, leaving a berm that ran almost down half the block. At its highest point, the berm was about two feet taller than me. Part of the back yard had grass. Dad had planted grass up next to the house. We didn't have grass in the back part of the yard next to the alley and woods. It looked like a huge sandbox between the back grass and the alley.

David, my five-year-old brother, was digging a hole in the sand when I left to cross the highway. Now he was covering it with dead tree branches he had dragged from the edge of the woods. I jumped off the berm onto the alley. Blackjack followed, passed me and ran into David's now deep hole. David, who was dragging another tree branch yelled "Hey, there's a dog in my fort."

David dropped to his knees to crawl into his fort while Blackjack barked at him. David stopped. When I got to them, I could see the dog, his head lowered and stretched forward, his tail held low and thumping, his eyes fixed on my little brother's eyes. Terrified, I knew I had to take control. If Blackjack bit David, Mom and Dad would never let me keep him. I just had to keep him. I yelled "Blackjack!" For only an instant the dog's eyes darted to mine, then back to David. I yelled louder. "Blackjack, come here!" I pointed down to my heel. He came; I kissed his head and scratched his ears. I was so relieved. David stood up and Blackjack thrust his forehead in David's belly, he laughed and scratched the dog.

Our sisters Susie and Deanna had come running when they heard the ruckus. Blackjack broke away from my side and ran circles around them until we were all standing at the entrance of David's fort. Susie was clearly delighted with the fort and the dog. Deanna sighed, rolled her eyes, and shook her head. "It's a dumb fort," she said. "It's going to rain and fill up with water, just like the Smiths' basement."

"Nice doggy, pretty doggy," Susie whispered into Blackjack's ear. Susie was tiny for a four-year-old. She squeezed her arms around his neck, rubbing her face in his fur. To my relief Blackjack was very gentle with her. "Can we keep it?" she asked.

"I don't know. We have to ask Mom and Dad" I said. "You stay here and play with him. I'm going to fix some lunch. We can eat in the fort, like a picnic."

Deanna followed me into the house and watched while I made sandwiches. I found an old oilcloth table cover for the fort floor. Deanna was six, she could be sneaky and could cry real tears whenever she wanted to get someone else in trouble. Mom and Dad thought she was very intelligent. I wondered if that was because she has had to wear glasses since she was four. Grandpa Diehl wore glasses from the drug store because someone told him his safety glasses made him look like an intellectual. Mostly, I thought Deanna was a smart aleck.

But sometimes, she was smart. Deanna looked straight at me and said, "Don't ask Mom. Ask Dad, before Mom gets home."

# Got Karma?

by Tim Montbriand

"You're gonna love this moving picture," everyone had told me, so I was excited when the curtains were drawn. The show, called "Got Karma" according to my wife, started slowly with views of distant mesas streaked brown, pink, and white like melting Neapolitan ice cream, and then panned quickly across miles and miles of barren and isolated desert scrub, green spots—they looked like tribbles—on the tan sand in the foreground.

The show then shifted to fleeting glimpses of slapped-together houses sheltered in the scattered copses of stunted trees. Some of the houses were intact; some had been reduced by weather and time to little more than a pile of fanned-out boards. The only signs of a human presence were the dusty old-model cars and the occasional repurposed school bus, its original color long since faded. Every so often, a stone building with no door or roof, some proud relic of the past, would enter the frame.

There was no complex musical soundtrack, just a rhythmic undertone complemented by haunting horn sounds barely audible. The artful presentation of very different vistas juxtaposed at varying speeds was music in itself, and whoever had created this presentation was as much a conductor as she was a director. I was increasingly intrigued and wondered what karmic message she wished to convey with the images. I knew that Buddhists believed an individual's actions in this earthly world determined his destiny/fate in the next stage of existence. But the show had not so far focused on any individuals.

The plains, dotted everywhere with cows, horses, and sheep, all with their young offspring, came next. The plains turned to farmland with fields of plowed brown earth checker-boarded with rolling hills of mown grass or incipient crops. I loved the close-ups of farm enclosures—the white clapboard main houses, the irregularly painted barns and utility sheds, and the haphazardly arranged tractors, trucks, and cars. I imagined the smell of hay and grass as I watched a handful of people in the yard moving about slowly but purposefully.

Then we saw crystalline, sapphire lakes glittering in the gaps of forests and were afforded an occasional glimpse of cautious wild animals at the forest's edge, the division between nature and civilization. There were cottages on the lakes, each with its own pier and safely secured powerboat. These cottages, no doubt, were the playgrounds of escape for rich folks from the city, a dramatic triumph over basic subsistence.

The director/conductor showed us American towns. Some were bustling with energy and had freshly paved and curbed streets, neat brick store facades, and manicured lawns. Newly erected franchise stores—Home Depot, Walmart, Dollar General—braced huge strip-mall parking lots with shiny new cars and their singularly focused, harried owners. Newly built gas station/markets and fast-food restaurants, constantly busy, littered every intersection.

Some towns were lethargic with potholed streets bordering on slowly decomposing houses crowded together on small lots and separated by chain link fences. The few scattered residents seemed without purpose, entering what looked like an old RXall drugstore or shepherding shabbily dressed children across a lonely railroad crossing to nowhere.

But it was always the backyards we were shown, the secret side of the owners' lives: the rusted bicycles, motorless cars up on cement blocks, and the discarded, newfangled inventions of the recent past— exercise bicycles, rowing machines, old, bulky, outdated television sets, blow-up pools dry and collapsed, crooked and battered aluminum sheds, mildewed mattresses, and dilapidated lawn furniture.

After a fleeting glimpse of a city skyline with its towering sky scrapers came scenes of the adjacent urban areas with their abandoned, vandalized buildings. Graffiti was everywhere and proclaimed a ghostlike victory of nihilism over order. Worse yet were the old factories barely functioning in the shadow of their glorious past—

dilapidated warehouses surrounded by a "mousetrap" of mysterious pipes.

No one seemed to be moving about in the warehouses, which were dark even though evidence of some enterprise was visible in the smoke that emanated from huge stacks. The dirty, neglected interiors of the warehouses made me feel sad for the lonely rearguard of workers who still trudged to work every day.

With lightning quickness, we were shown rows and rows of rusted railcars stretching for miles. Some of the railcars were tank-shaped with "Edible Tallow" written on the sides, "Animal Fat" in parentheses, and I remembered the prancing colts and calves from the plains.

The picture show ended with the darkness of a cavernous underground. I was immensely pleased with my insight into the message of the tour-de-force moving picture show: The director/conductor was not addressing the karma of the individual, but that of all humankind, and she had brilliantly presented us with a graphic understanding of the inevitable entropy that plagues civilizations, a kind of evolutionary karma in which all human creations inevitably crumble as described in Shelley's poem "Ozymandias."

With a flurry of activity and a thirst for glory, humankind abandons the comfortable routines of nature and builds great monuments, forgetting, or never realizing beforehand, that those monuments need to be maintained with the same amount of energy as was expended in the original build. I thought back to the show's contrasts between the natural world of forests/plains and the domesticated farmland; between the bustling cities and dying towns; between the great manufacturing age and its decaying, polluting aftermath. Maybe the show's message was that karma for humankind would be to live close to nature and be happy in this existence and the next.

I followed the crowd to the lit-up area beneath a brightly lit sign: CHICAGO UNION STATION—*GO AMTRAK*.

I turned with a smile toward my wife, who had once asked me why a street performer had placed a "spit" bucket in front of his audience. I said, "Got karma? That's a good one," kidding her as I often did about her occasional and mildly dyslexic moments.

"What goes around comes around," she said. "And trains are kinda like that. I just wanted you to know."

Flash prompt: Vanilla Cokes and Jukeboxes

# Johnny Angel
## by Pat Leso

Life is what happens between the dates on a tombstone. That dash is life. The dates are only the start and end of the race.

Songs have a life too. They bring back memories like vanilla cokes, "Johnny Angel" playing on the jukebox, and sitting in the malt shop with your best friends.

That's how it all started. The perfect guy walked over to her table and said, "Susie, could I talk to you a minute?"

"Sure, Johnny," Susie said. Her friends giggled.

"Privately." He held out his hand. They walked outside past the picture window. He hemmed and hawed, finally stopped and sputtered, "Will you go to the prom with me?"

Inside, she silently screamed, yes, yes, yes! On the outside, she calmly looked into his eyes and said, "Yes, that would be wonderful."

"Good. That's swell. Let me know what color dress you'll be wearing, and my mom will get a matching corsage."

"Alright."

"Well now that that's settled, let me take you back to your friends. I've got to get to work."

Susie smiled. "I'll see you tomorrow."

"Yep."

*****

She kissed his lips. "I love you, but it's time to go. You've lingered long enough. Don't worry about me. I'll be alright. Just don't go dancing with anyone else. I'll be there before you know it."

Sixty-six years, four months, and twelve days. *We had a great life together*. She never forgot that date. She told him she loved him one last time and held his hand as he left.

She put the flowers on his grave.

Flash prompt: Vanilla Cokes and Jukeboxes

## Last Visit to Sid's
by T.A. Novak

I slid into a booth at Sid's Diner. Sid's is one of those retro, shiny-aluminum, dining-car burger joints that have been fading into the sunset.

Susie came by and plopped a glass of ice water in front of me. "Pepsi," I said.

"We only have Coke products," she answered with a smirk. "Sid got a better price from the Coke guy."

"Okay, a Coke then." I looked at the menu on the wall. "And two coney dogs."

I was glad the Seeburg Wall-O-Matic was still in each booth. *Changes, too many changes*, I thought as I flipped through the tabs. *Thank God some of the old favorites are still here.* "Blue Suede Shoes" and "You Ain't Nothing, but a Hound Dog" were under the Elvis tab. The main jukebox was moaning "Your Cheatin' Heart."

I craned my neck, and sure enough, there was that wanna-be country singer, Harry, making small talk with my waitress. I wondered how many quarters he fed the jukebox. When would I hear something more palatable?

I flipped the tabs on my table-top jukebox, searching for the perfect song for Harry. Something not so twangy.

Susie was back. "I got you the new Coke flavor, vanilla."

"I wanted a cola flavor."

"I guess you won't like our turkey dogs then either."

"Not Koegels?"

"We don't carry Koegels anymore."

I found the perfect song for Harry, punched in L-7, and left Sid's without eating, drinking, or paying. "Bubba Shot the Jukebox" was playing. I smiled.

Flash prompt: Vanilla Cokes and Jukeboxes

## "Whenever I Want You"
### by Karen VanderJagt

Sherry came every Friday night to the Crossroads Diner. The owners always saved the back corner table, and her cheeseburger, fries, and vanilla coke were on the house. Though only a child, I watched her sit in solitude, and my heart hurt. One Friday, I tried to approach her but was shooed away by the waitress. I saw Sherry press B-10 on the table jukebox and the smooth sounds of the Everly Brothers serenaded her.

"What's her story?" I asked the waitress years later when overcome by my teenage curiosity.

"She's waiting for her fiancé, Donny Adams, to return. That was their spot," the waitress said.

"Return from where?"

"Korea."

"But that war ended years ago."

"We know, but he never came home."

"Killed in action?"

"No, missing."

Sherry continued her ritual until the diner was sold and the jukeboxes disappeared. I sometimes wondered what had happened to her until I saw a small article in the local paper. Some remains returned by North Korea were identified as those of Private Donny Adams, KIA in 1952. Burial would be Friday night, June 7, 2002.

I went to the cemetery to pay my respects and watched as Sherry sat among family and friends. After everyone else had left, she pulled out her cassette player and pushed the button. I hadn't heard that song since the diner.

"Whenever I want you, all I have to do is dream, dream, dream dream. . ."

Sherry may not have gotten her dream, but at least she got an answer.

Flash Prompt: Cupid Unrestrained

## The Hand of Gramma Cupie
by Jane Schopen

"Kat, can you talk?"

"Yeah, what's up, Zach? You sound weird."

"Well, I've had my mind blown by the picture you just instagrammed."

"The one of me at Disney World as a kid?"

"Yeah, How old were you then?"

"Um, seven, I think. I *was* totally adorable. Were you smitten? Is that what blew you away?"

"Did you live in Florida back then?" asked Zach.

"No, we went there for one of my dad's work conferences. We were so psyched to go to Disney World. Such a great trip."

"I'm trying to figure this out. My grandma didn't live there either. Did you ever meet my Gramma Cupie?"

"I don't think so. Zach, what are you trying to figure out?"

"That Gramma never knew you. You and I have been friends since…"

"Tenth grade. Wait, is this the matchmaker grandma you joke about? I *wish* I'd met her."

"Kat, she was relentless. That's why we called her Gramma Cupie—short for Cupid. She was forever telling people who they should or shouldn't be dating. It was weird and maddening especially because she was almost always right on."

"What does this have to do…?"

"Look at your Disney picture again. That is my Gramma Cupie standing behind you!"

"The lady with the crazy hair and the heart balloon?"

"Yes, she's unmistakable. I'm telling you *it's her* twenty years ago."

"Oh my God. That's so . . ."

"One more question, Kat."
"What?"
"Would you consider going out with me, like on a date?"

Flash prompt: Booze Cruise

## If Mamma Don't Sleep

by Jane Schopen

"Read between the lines," Artie growled, jabbing three middle fingers towards his bar mates. He glowered back at them as he shuffled out the door, listing to one side. Mr. Earl's had been his third and final stop of the evening. He knew when to head home.

None of those drunk degenerates appreciated his deep insights about the woes of the world. Two younger fellows had acted like Heckle and Jeckle, rigging his barstool to malfunction and yukking it up when he face-planted. Then the smarmy barkeep refused to hand over his keys and told him, "Walk if off or call an Uber goober."

Artie cursed the bad chip seal and ice that made him slip and fall all the way to his dark house. He banged on the door forever before his wife, Mary, opened it. She looked bad--rumpled and sleepy. She hadn't looked good for a long time, so he owed it to her to enumerate his many concerns.

When he arrived at his chief complaint, "You got fat, Mary. I can tolerate ugly, but not fat," she hollered back, "Shut up and let me sleep. I gotta work a double today."

Artie kicked their smelly hound off the couch, flopped down, and passed out. An alarm woke him. Mary didn't turn it off, so she must have left for work. He couldn't find the damned clock, but it finally stopped. Five minutes later, another alarm went off. He covered his aching head but still heard the TV and radio jump to high-volume life. Soon the stove alarm blared.

# Greenhorn at Green Acres
## by Tim Montbriand

When I graduated from my affluent suburban high school, my old man would come home from work every day and say, "When the hell are you gonna get off your ass and get a job? I worked two jobs when I was your age." Well I got tired of that pretty quick, so I answered an ad calling for an "energetic youth to work on an organic farm" and, to my dismay, was hired.

The morning I showed up for work I knew exactly what was going on. A couple from the suburbs had bought an old farm and were aiming to grow their own food and raise their own animals so they could be sure never again to ingest harmful chemicals. They reminded me of Oliver and Lisa from the television show "Green Acres," and that's what I called them.

Oliver still worked in the city and drove sixty miles roundtrip every day, so Lisa was the boss. My first job was to clean the barn floor, which was piled three feet high in old straw and cow shit, and spread the manure on their huge garden. Before I could start, I had to hook up a wagon to the tractor, which had the trailer hitch on the front. *Who the hell puts a trailer hitch on the front?* I tried driving forward, but after three near-catastrophic jackknives, I just drove backwards. *Yeah, this is what a real farmhand does; this looks impressive.*

Pitchforking the barn manure didn't seem bad. There was a sweet smell of warm hay coming from the barn loft and the flattened cow dung had an inoffensive, earthy tang. After a couple of hours, though, the job seemed unending, like one of the twelve tasks of Hercules—cleaning the Augean Stables—and I was looking around for a river to divert through the barn's big double doors.

Lisa saved me. "Come on," she said. "You can take a break from this and clean out the two horse stalls." *Oh, that's great! It's good to vary different kinds of animal shit.*

She took me to the stalls and said, "I'll check on you in a bit." I thought she was making a pun, but she walked away.

"Hey," I called. "Aren't you going to remove the horses?"

"Oh, they won't hurt you. Just don't spook 'em, and if they act up, give 'em a whack." *Right, I'll kick their asses for sure.* Man, those road apples smelled, looked, and sounded nasty as they tumbled into the wheelbarrow.

I got a break from shoveling shit the next day when Lisa brought old Doctor Evans out to see if the Charolais beef cow was pregnant. The doc was about eighty years old, thin and fragile. He and Lisa led the huge cow out into the yard, and the doc told me to hold tight to its halter. Then Doc Evans stuck his arm up the cow's ass to check the uterus. The Charolais knocked the doctor down and dragged me ten feet before I could release the halter. When Lisa helped the doc off the ground, his glasses were broken and hanging from one ear. He looked at me and said, "I told you to hold her!" He shook his head in disbelief at my failure and said, "Let's put it in the barn's stanchion." *Hey, that's a good idea. Put the eight-hundred-pound cow in a metal stanchion before we goose her. Who would've thought?*

One morning, Lisa and I tried to load two pigs onto her pickup truck and take them to the butcher. The pigpen was a sludgy pond of mud and manure. I quickly discovered that pigs cannot be herded like cattle. Lisa and I linked arms trying to direct them to the truck, but they were lightning fast at changing directions. When one of the pigs ran back into its stall, I grabbed a wooden pallet and tried to push it back outside, but the damned thing did an about-face and squeezed through the boards.

We chased and dove after them until we were splattered with mud and fecal sludge. Then Lisa said, "I'm gonna call Herb; he raises pigs and took ours to market last year." *What a novel idea, Lisa—getting an expert to corral these pigs.*

Herb showed up and backed his truck into position. He took a bucket, put it over the first pig's head, grabbed its tail, and backed it up onto the truck. Herb repeated the procedure with the second pig. It took him about ten minutes. I couldn't believe what I had just seen.

My last day on the farm we were to kill and clean chickens and put them in the freezer. Inside the coop, the chickens started flying around and screeching. The minute Lisa caught one, though, the others landed and started creeping around emitting sympathetic moans. We caught a dozen, tied their legs together, and hung them in a tree. Lisa directed me to behead the first chicken on a nearby stump. The hatchet was dull and made the poor bird groan. I hacked away as humanely as possible then sharpened the hatchet, dispatched the rest of the chickens, and hung them back on the tree to bleed out. Things then went from disgusting to insufferable. We took the birds to a cellar, and Lisa showed me how to empty a chicken's craw. She then plunged the bird into a pot of boiling water to make it easier to pull the quills. The smell was hideous, and after controlling my retching I said, "Lisa, why do you do this? You know you can buy chickens cleaned and wrapped at the grocery store? You can even buy just those parts of the chicken you like most."

Maybe it was my impertinence or my general ineptitude, but Lisa spat out, "We won't be needing you here anymore, Greenhorn."

It's funny that of all the jobs I've had Green Acres is the one I think of most often and most fondly.

# Albina

by Mary Corrao

It rained the day of my mother's funeral. A sea of umbrellas surrounded the gravesite. When the sea parted and the mourners moved toward their cars, I noticed a limo parked farther away. A young man exited the sleek black vehicle, approached me, handed me a note, then quickly retreated to the dry haven of the vehicle, and drove off.

*I am sorry for your loss. Please call me. Your mother's friend, Albina.*

At the bottom of the note was her number. Her name resurrected a memory sealed and now reopened.

When I was a child, a woman named Albina periodically visited my mother. My mind's photo was of a large regal woman with a kind, pretty face. She was always impeccably dressed in navy blue, her makeup perfectly blended into her smooth skin. She wore a unique perfume, which both preceded her and left a trail behind. She came bearing gifts of chocolate lollipops.

Albina's visits were unexpected. My mother was always in the midst of chores when she arrived. Dressed in a loose-fitting housedress, hair unkept, no makeup, she was the antithesis of her visitor. I sensed an oddness in their relationship, my mother continuing her housework, Albina sitting like royalty in our tiny tenement apartment.

She never stayed longer than an hour, never came when my father was home, never attended social get-togethers with family and friends.

At the age of nine, we moved to the suburbs, and I never saw Albina again until the morning we buried my mother.

Consumed by curiosity, I called her the next morning and made a date to meet her at the penthouse apartment on the Upper West Side of Manhattan. At the door, a middle-aged woman led the way to a richly decorated but cozy living room. There sat Albina. She had to be in her nineties, but despite some wrinkles, she was still the woman I remembered, her perfume filling the air.

"I'll waste no time because at the age of ninety-two with Alzheimer's at my door, I have no time to mince words," she said. "I've done a terrible, terrible thing. Before my memories blow away, I need to tell someone. Since it involves your mother, Anna, you should know."

Astonishment prevented my thoughts from seeping out of my mouth. What would a woman I hardly knew confess to me, and how was my mother involved?

She continued without missing a beat. "I killed a man, and your mother and I hid the body."

For a split second, my life felt like a lie as I sat open-mouthed before this strange woman. Seeing my face, she laughed like a person more wicked than first impressions revealed. Was she pulling my leg?

Just then she received a call. "I must go," she said. "Come back tomorrow, and I will explain it all."

Because that is the way life works, I was called out of town on business the next day. When I returned the following week, Albina had taken ill and was in the hospital. After several months, she was moved to a private nursing home. Her illness sped up her mental decline. By the time I saw her again, she had begun the final, harrowing descent of her mind.

In what sometimes seemed like lucid moments, she gathered her thoughts and spouted a jumble of information. "When you love someone, you'll do almost anything to keep them. There is nothing good about getting old, my dear. I'd chosen the life I belonged to. I am desperate, Anna. He will tell William everything. He will ruin my marriage. I should have felt guilt for what I did, but it's not there."

She moved from young to old, now to then, strong to vulnerable.

Over several months, I watched her slip from forgetting to babbling to silence.

Six months after Albina had crept back into my life, I left her room for the last time. Before I walked out, her eyes transformed for an instant into those of her younger self. They moved sideways to a box.

Did I imagine a faint smile as I opened the box of chocolate lollipops? When I looked at her again, the glimmer was gone, and nothing remained but the lingering perfume.

Albina died the next day and with her the untold truth. Was it just the imaginings of an old woman? I would never know.

Closing my eyes, I gave my head a shake, sucked on a chocolate lollipop, and opened the bottle of my unique perfume.

# An Escape to Freedom
## by T.A. Novak

Lucia was rolled into a tight ball under her father's workbench where he had pushed her at the sound of the first shot. "Get down, baby girl," he had shouted. Dozens of gunshots, maybe a hundred, followed.

Her father, Diego Hernandez, had been showing his son Pablo how to start stitching a new pair of boots he was making. When Lucia dared open her eyes, pieces of sheetrock and wood were still drifting down upon her, and she could feel the weight of her father lying across her legs. *He's a cobbler. How can this be happening?*

When the gunfire stopped, Lucia could hear the moans of the dying and wounded. There were no sirens, no police, no ambulances. She freed her legs and looked at her father. "Papa," she wailed. Her father lay on his back, blood seeping from the corner of his mouth and his eyes wide open in death. In his right hand, he was clutching his cobbler's awl, a tool his father had given him many years before.

She sat upright. Near the doorway to the plaza was her younger brother Paulo. He too lay dead. She fought back the tears as she sobbed deeply. *No, I must be strong.*

Lucia knew scenes like this were all too common in San Pedro Sula, Honduras. It would be an hour or two before any authorities would dare to stick their heads out. Unfortunately, her father and thirteen-year-old brother happened to be in the wrong place at the wrong time—the family's cobbler shop.

She calmly stood, dusted herself off, and walked to her family's living quarters in the back of the shop. She showered, dressed for the trek north, and filled her backpack with essentials. As she packed, she found her mother's black rosary. It was the only thing she had from a mother who had died when Lucia was four. She was now eighteen. Many times before, she had thought of leaving Honduras, but her father and brother had needed her. They no longer did.

She removed the family's funds hidden under the floorboards in the kitchen. The last thing she did was pry the cobbler's awl from her father's hand. She walked to the bus station and bought a ticket to Mexico.

Lucia Hernandez was fleeing to a destination she had only read about, the United States, intent on making her way by bus. So she had dressed as plainly as she could: baggy jeans and a baggy top. Growing up, she had been called a *Mestiza,* which meant she was of Indian and European heritage. She had jet-black hair, dark brown eyes, flawless skin, and beautiful facial features. But, all too soon, she would discover that her natural beauty was a magnet to unwanted advances.

Traveling by bus was a slow way to travel north, but the cheapest. On one bone-jarring ride across the state of Chiapas, Mexico, five male travelers had tried starting a conversation with Lucia. One, in particular, followed her while on a stopover in the small town of Escuintla. The evening darkness must have emboldened the man, and he attacked her as she left a small CARNICERÍA, a delicatessen, to head back to her bus. He threw her to the ground. To his surprise, her hand found a rock as she struggled to push him off. She hit him once in his left eye and again in his forehead. She hit him again for good measure. His blood started pooling under his head as Lucia stood, picked up her packages, and walked away.

She boarded her bus, looking forward to the burrito and the Jarritos orange soda she had purchased at the store where she had also picked up a copy of *Dario La Prensa,* the San Pedro Sula newspaper. She wanted something to read as she traveled. It would be a long night to the next stop in the state of Oaxaca.

The uneven highway and memories of the attack would not let her sleep, so she opened the newspaper. Tucked away on the third page was an article headlined, "Turf War Battle." The report read, "On September 10, 2020, MS thirteen gang members opened fire in front of a shoe shop in the Honduran city of San Pedro Sula, one hundred miles north of Tegucigalpa. The town is a place known to be a base for cocaine refining operations. The dispute, thought to be over drug territories threatened by a rival gang, left seventeen people dead." There was no mention of her father, her brother, or any other innocent people killed. Instead, all were lumped into the final tally of seventeen dead.

Lucia took a few deep breaths, whispering "El descanso Eterno les concede, oh Señor—*Eternal rest grant unto them O Lord,"* and cried. She fell asleep repeating that prayer over and over while thumbing the beads on her mother's rosary.

Lucia rode what was commonly called "chicken buses," a name given to recycled yellow school buses from Canada and the USA used as public transport in much of Central America and Mexico. They are gaudily painted vehicles with short and inexpensive routes. At the end of one route, travelers waited for another chicken bus. Somebody tried attacking Lucia numerous times during her trek. The second attack occurred on the outskirts of Mexico City, another on El Camino Real in Monterrey, and another on the side streets of Durango and Sonora, Mexico. Because of the first attack, she kept her father's tool handy. The cobbler's awl ended these attacks efficiently. She didn't know if any of her attackers died but knew for sure they were hurt and had bled.

Other travelers told Lucia aboard the different buses making the same trek that coyotes would seek her out and transport her across the border for a fee. One old man warned her, "Negotiate, but watch for thieves and murderers." So she kept the awl very close. It was hidden inconspicuously under her blouse on her right side, with the pointed end slipped under her belt, its tee handle holding it in place.

Early in her travels, she had found a sarape abandoned under a seat on one of the chicken buses she rode. She kept it, knowing the nights could get cold in the desert. It worked as a shawl or as her bed as the weeks dragged on. It also came in handy to disguise her appearance if needed.

In San Luis Rio Colorado, Sonora, Mexico, she abandoned her bus, following a group with the same intentions she had. Lucia walked until she and the others found a makeshift encampment. Yuma, Arizona, was rumored to be close. The camp was a stop the coyotes would often check for travelers. Corrugated pieces of tin nailed to trees slowed the winds and provided some shade, but not much else. She had picked a hollowed-out area littered with empty water bottles and food wrappers, cleaning it up as best as possible. She only needed a place to sleep.

Lucia had walked a half-day and was taking a siesta when she heard a voice. "Senorita, come quickly; I take you."

Another man, resting nearby under a beat-up straw hat, heard the invitation and caught Lucia's eye as she gathered her belongings. He shook his head at her, but she started following the man.

"Take me too," the man with the straw hat said. "I go too."

"No, no. The senorita first."

Lucia followed the man leading her through mesquite trees, creosote bushes, and cholla. She wasn't one hundred yards from her nest when he turned on her, throwing her to the ground. As he jumped on her, she thrust three quick jabs with her right fist into his midsection. The man yelped, rolling onto his back screaming, "Puta," and went silent. Within Lucia's fist was the awl. The six-inch narrow point protruded out between her middle and ring finger. The man's blood painted her fist.

She jumped when she heard a twig snap. The man that had been napping near her looked down at the attacker and smiled. "I guess you didn't need my help, senorita." He helped gather her things and handed them to her. "Coyotes move people in the night." He grabbed the man's ankles and dragged the body farther away from the encampment without another word. Lucia stood and watched.

In ten minutes, he returned. "Let's go back, senorita. The coyotes will come in the darkness. Tonight, we cross the border."

Lucia followed the man at a safe distance. She didn't recognize his accent. But by his dark hair, eyes, and facial features, she knew he was not from Honduras or Guatemala. *Mexican, maybe?*

Lucia rested but did not sleep. The man under the straw hat occupied her thoughts. He did not look like the many men she had seen making the journey north. Yes, he had been out in the weather like her, unbathed, unshaven, and in rags. But he was different. Young and strong. She didn't let the word *kind* creep into her thoughts. She was travelling in a very hostile world and was praying that life in the United States would be different.

There are reasons people like her undertake an arduous journey—living on a dream, sometimes even finding death.

Flash prompt: The One That Got Away

## A Killer Smile
### by Mary Corrao

Death pays my bills. Virtue doesn't accumulate wealth. Being a hit woman was simply a job, a job at which I excelled. Kai always said I had a soul with no boundaries and a killer smile.

Kai and I spent two years together in a foster home with four other kids. His name means beauty, and to me he was that and more. My life was devoid of love except for our time together. Tall, angular, clever, and brazen, he had a scar across his cheek, which instead of diminishing his beauty, made him more remarkable.

We shared the life of the neglected and unwanted. He nicknamed me Snow White because of my alabaster skin, which contrasted with his chocolate exterior. We blended our colors and our bodies in the field behind the house. I knew from the beginning that he would be the best and worst thing ever to happen to me. He proved me right the night he snuck away, leaving me behind.

I'd chosen the life I instinctively belonged to. It came naturally to me, which made me the best in the business. Tonight's job should have been routine; then, I caught a rear view of the scoundrel of color.

"So, they sent Snow White," he said as he slowly turned to face me, gun pointing at my chest.

My mind sharpened to caffeine alertness. My mouth flashed a smile. My gun was on the ready.

Life and death were milliseconds apart in the gap of silence between whatever happened before and what was to come.

Flash prompt: The One That Got Away

## Bytes Dog Man

by Tim Montbriand

The instructional technology (IT) unit of the college had been moved to a small unused classroom, and the IT techs were lunching there and sharing the latest news. The senior tech behind a cluttered desk had two other techs laughing.

"We've been paperless here for eighteen months, and old Doctor Laurence is still writing his lectures on the white board, in cursive, and the students are complaining. So Dean Jones writes a service ticket directing me to show the old codger how to put his notes up on the projector—she's been on his case for months—and how to use the new laptop she's giving him. So I go to his classroom this morning and try to walk him through the process. He can't even understand the basics of what I'm showing him, and he starts yammering, in his elegant English accent, about how students depend too much on technology:

'They take pictures of my lecture notes on the board, and they can't commit anything to memory. I remind them that Homer and other bards committed epics to memory, and I tell them that information in the memory, unlike googled information, is active and readily available to make connections with information from new experiences.'

I know my mission is futile, so I hand him his new laptop and inform him that it's got 128 megabytes and will help him organize all of his stuff.

'But how will this thing help me do that?' he asked.

With an app, I tell him, and he says,

'Yes; I've known a good nap to help sort things.'

And then the old fart asks, 'What's a byte?'

So I explain. It's eight bits, you know, binary ones and zeros, and then when he frowns, I add, it's the future, Doc, you can't get away from it. Then he says; 'I think one could very well get away from it,' and I want to say, yeah, you old curmudgeon, but if one gets away, all that's left is a big fat zero."

Flash prompt: The One That Got Away

# The One That Got A Weigh
## by Jim Veary

Nancy Scovil began the day with a nervous stomach. She considered sticking her finger down her throat to end the anxiety once and for all, but she hated throwing up even more than she hated this unreasoning fear that always gripped her on Wednesdays.

Her paltry breakfast was just going to have to stay where it was. She checked herself in the mirror, didn't like what she saw, but looked decent enough to leave the house.

Nancy got to her meeting early, before the line snaked completely around the perimeter of the large room. Her empty stomach was audibly moaning.

She reached the head of the line and started her routine. Shoes came off as well as her ankle socks and the pretty silver ankle bracelet. She placed the bracelet in her purse, followed by her rings and watch, and put the purse on a table beside her. She unclipped her earrings and hair clip and dropped them into the open bag. Next, she removed her sweater, careful not to raise the light cotton dress she was wearing. She was commando underneath—no bra, no panties.

The fear climaxed as she stepped up onto the scale. The digital display flickered then settled in at 199.9. Her heart leaped in her chest. She had done it—Hallelujah ; she was under two hundred.

As she gathered up her things, she thought she should celebrate after the Weight Watchers' meeting with a hot fudge sundae at Denny's.

Flash prompt: Guilty Pleasures

# Guilty Plea? Sure!
## by Tim Montbriand

Ms. McRae gives us prisoners prompts, and we can write anything in response. When she said, "Today's prompt is 'guilty pleasures'; I know that's an *oxymoron* . . ." Big Wayne yelled, "She insulted me. I'm addicted. I ain't writin' nothin'." Me, I'm the Shawshank Shakespeare, and I wrote the poem below:

**Guilty Plea? Sure!**
Some guys thrill at sneaking a piece of cake
That doctors say is not good for their health.
Some others like to drive out to a lake
And wait 'til dark to skinny dip with stealth.
Some folks, I've heard, will never fail to take
Hotel towels despite their own great wealth.

I really feel that guilt's the same as pleasure
'Cause it feels good to key some bastard's Benz.
There's no way that you can ever measure
The thrill I get while casing joints with friends.
We grab and run and make off with the treasure.
We break and enter and never make amends.

I often shoot out windows just for fun,
Forcing some poor slob to make repairs.
You know, it's really fun to shoot a gun.
It's just a plate of glass; who really cares?
When I hit a store and the booty's won,
I know I've done what weakling never dares.

Sometimes we're caught and do a stint in jail,
School for learning new techniques in crime.
Every single inmate has a tale
'Bout what went wrong to make him serve his time.
We're all so sure that we will soon get bail
And ne'er again do a nickel or dime.

**Disclaimer:**
If any reader thinks that he might thrive
By ratting me out while I am still alive,
I'll just plead Amendment Number Five.

Flash prompt: Solving the World's Problems at the Sportsman's Cafe

## A Simple Solution
by Beverly Jackson

Four men, older than dirt, congregate each morning at eight A.M. sharp in the Sportsman's Cafe. All four sit in the same booth: Old George and Sloppy Joe on one side and Cudger Coot and Smitty Jones on the other. Each huddles over his mug of steeping hot Joe, and each grumbles about the world's problems, but today they end their talk by speaking about their wives.

Old George spoke first. "Ya know what? I shoulda divorced my ol' lady before I got too old. Now it's too late. We're too ancient and too hurtin' to do nuthin' about it."

"Oh, I can do ya one better," piped up Sloppy Joe. "My wife divorced me, took all our money, and sold our house. I'm broke *and* homeless."

Cudger Coot, not wanting to be outdone, joined in with his tale of woe. "You two live on Easy Street. My wife hates my guts so much she divorced me but still *lives* with me. Says she's gonna enjoy spending the rest of her life making mine a living hell."

Smitty Jones remained quiet, listening to his friends complain, a Mona Lisa smile plastering his lips. The other three noticed and stared at him until he finally spoke.

"I have a fruit tree in my backyard that bears gorgeous crops each year. Turns out my Lucy Ann makes a wonderful fertilizer."

Flash prompt: Guilty Pleasures

## Justice is in the Bite

by Beverly Jackson

They say pigs will eat anything. Such are the thoughts that ran through my mind this morning. Me and my wife have farmed this land for years. Chores are done without giving them much mind, giving me plenty of room to think of ordinary and not-so-ordinary stuff.

Two months ago, while I was bailing hay, I was thinking of my beautiful wife, Jenny, and how happy our lives were right up 'till John Joseph Templeton bought the farm closest to ours. There was something about him I didn't like. Our small town is tight, and we all help one another. John Joseph Templeton was a little too helpful, especially where Jenny was concerned.

Last month, I was herding the cows to barn for milking and found Jenny crying. Her dress was torn, and when I tried to comfort her, she pulled away. She told me Mr. Templeton had raped her. We went to the police and filed a complaint, and Jenny was taken to the hospital, but here it is four weeks later, and the police state that there is nothing they can do. "Lack of evidence," they said.

Today, I have just finished feeding my pigs. I sit here and watch, wondering how long it will take them to finish John Joseph Templeton. I do hope me and Jenny can get through this. Yes, I am guilty of murder, but with no proof I doubt I'll be convicted. The pleasure is all mine.

Flash prompt: Lost in Memories

## And Then There Was One
by Pat Leso

    Her mind wandered while the man droned on and on at the podium. Suzie had met him thirty minutes before, but she couldn't remember his name. Her brain was on vacation from this life; only her body was in the room.

    His voice had an almost hypnotizing lilt to it as he talked about life. At least that's how Suzie thought he sounded. She really wasn't paying attention. Her headache kept pounding between her eyes, and it took everything she had to keep from throwing up where she sat.

    Time no longer had meaning. Sleep eluded her. Nightmares haunted her dreams. She woke up in a cold sweat, afraid to close her eyes again. Death was calling her. She was only nineteen.

    Ralph, her older brother, sat next to her while the man continued with his sermon. Suzie knew Ralph was worried just by his non-stop tapping on her leg, as if doing Morse code. She wanted him to stop but was afraid to open her mouth.

    Friends were worried too. They'd stop by Suzie's home often to check on her. She'd smile and say she was fine, but they could see the bags under her eyes.

    Phone calls went unanswered; she was too tired to make small talk. All she wanted was to find peace.

    Staring off into the distance, Suzie started to daydream of better times: school dances, beach trips, and her wedding. Life was one big party until it wasn't.

    The pastor stopped speaking. In a loud voice he said, "Let us pray for Joshua Alexander Murphy, who left this world too soon. There will be full Military Funeral Honors at the gravesite for this brave soldier."

    The Military Guard was ready. Shots were fired into the air. The ceremonial folding and presentation of the flag was a moving sight.

When they handed her the flag while Taps played, her tears flowed. It was time to bury Suzie's husband.

She patted her stomach.

# His Final Epitaph
## by Karen VanderJagt

A spaceship is an expensive coffin.

Timothy looked out the port windows. The stars seemed extra bright in this section of sky. The brief flash of an icy blue comet passed by the window, and he strained to follow the glow of its tail. He'd seen a lot of comets in this system since his engines died a week before. Timothy credited luck for his continuing survival.

As scout for this solar system, Timothy searched for planets that were either suitable for colonization or were sources of raw materials for mining. So far, this sector had proved to be a bust with only one measly asteroid showing any promise.

He was just considering a return to base when the long-range scanner picked up a strong reading for gold, still one of the most valuable metals, and also a strange reading indicating an unknown material. Timothy altered course to investigate further. As he approached the planet, he was able to fine tune the location to one of the small moons orbiting the gas giant. As he decelerated to enter an orbit, a large plume of gas erupted from the giant. The gas enveloped his ship, and the engine died, snuffed out like a candle. Gas flooded the engine compartment and began to eat away at the core. Impurities in the gas trapped within began to coat the walls, solidifying as the substance melded with the metal.

Timothy knew that if he didn't get out of the toxic emissions, he was dead. In desperation, he launched a small missile into the cloud and detonated it. The explosion, much greater than he had anticipated, ignited the fumes and blew the ship away from the cloud by the force of the concussion wave.

When Timothy came to, he found the ship tumbling through the black and the gas giant no longer visible even on his radar. He did a systems check to confirm what he already knew. He was dead in the black. Life support was on standby and would carry him for a few weeks; food and water were good if he rationed, but without rescue, he was dead.

Timothy put his SOS on a continuous transmission until the dwindling battery power forced him to conserve. Then he could only send sporadic messages, hoping that someone would hear, futile as that might be. This section of the galaxy was not well traveled. His only real hope was that his failure to report in or return on schedule would launch a search.

For ten days, Timothy floated. He kept a meticulous log. After all, his job was about discovery, a solitary pursuit but one he found exciting. He started writing to friends and family. He wrote about his memories. He wrote about his feelings. He wrote things he never would have said to anyone, but now in the solitude of his floating coffin, he found he needed to say these things. After all, this would be all they'd have to remember him by.

On day twelve, the cluster came. For days he watched the comets fly by his view screen. Frightening and beautiful, their multicolored glows passed by his ship. Every color of the rainbow burned past. He was filled with wonder that such brilliant colors could fill the total black.

On day sixteen, they stopped, and he breathed a sigh of relief but also of regret. The comets had been his only companions. He cut back his rations again so that he got only twelve ounces of water and one meal pack each day. The radio broadcast his SOS for only one hour during that cycle.

On day twenty-one, he was down to eight ounces and a third of a meal pack. His uniform hung off his shoulders, and his belt was notched with extra holes. The air was stale, and he pulled out his EVA tanks to increase the oxygen level.

On day twenty-three, static sounded over his radio. He could make out a call but couldn't understand the words. He shouted into the mic and prayed. Pulling out his log, he noted the exact time. They couldn't be that far away. He was going to make it! Static sounded again and sounded frantic. He could just make out a few barely intelligible words. He looked out his port window to see if he could see the ship, but he couldn't. All he could see was the large comet heading straight for him. His luck had run out.

The Klaxon research ship, Ort, had been following the comet for the past two cycles trying to develop a plan to save their world. The mass of the icy rock was too great to be destroyed by their weapons, and there was not enough time to evacuate more than a token of their population. Hope dwindled to a fatalistic acceptance of the destruction of their home, their culture, their lives. They'd be a dying people floating in space without a planet.

"Leader, we have a transmission from an alien vessel in the path of the 'Destroyer,'" the communications officer reported.

"What does it say?" the leader asked.

"We haven't received enough for the translator to understand, seems to be repeating. Also, we are getting no power signature."

"Can we get to him in time?"

"No, Leader."

The Ort could only watch as the comet continued straight toward the unlucky ship.

"Another victim of the 'Destroyer,' " the Leader murmured. "Reverse course. We can't afford to be hit by debris."

Timothy grabbed his writings, placed them in an ore container and jettisoned them. Then he could do nothing more, watching in fascination as his death approached.

"How beautiful," he whispered to the swirling colors.

He never felt the massive explosion as the comet hit and the core ignited, amplified greatly by the substance coating the reactor. The comet changed course by a fraction of a degree. Timothy's tribute.

The Ort watched on the long-range scanner as the scout ship disintegrated in a large fiery burst of swirling reds, blues, and greens.

"Should we check out the debris field to see if anything survived?" the first officer said.

"Nothing survived that. Set course back to Klaxon."

"Leader, the translator says that ship was called Poe and there was only one crewman, a Timothy Hawthorne."

"Very well. Make a note in the log."

"Leader, Leader," an excited navigation officer shouted.

"What is it?" the tired Leader asked.

"The comet's course altered...by 0.9 degrees," he reported.

Stunned, the Leader replied, "Is it enough?"

"Yes, Leader, it is. It is."

The command center burst into cheers. After a moment, the Leader stopped, bowed his head, and the others followed his lead. Their world would live because Poe had died.

Unnoticed, Timothy's writings floated away.

# High and Dry
## by Tim Montbriand

"Let's check out the freak house first," Craig, my best friend and longtime schoolmate, shouted as we pulled into the parking lot of the Michigan State Fairgrounds. He was shouting against the temporary hearing loss we had incurred while cruising Woodward Avenue in the blue Mustang convertible his parents had given their only child on his eighteenth birthday.

"Let's get the lay of the land first," I said. I was excited. The sounds of human activity in the distance had always had a magnetic pull on me much like, I suppose, the cry of wolves or birds to their own species, announcing the opportunity to inspect and possibly interact.

We walked fast to the entrance, and the first amusement we encountered was the dunk tank. A man wearing a tuxedo and top hat sat in a cage on a collapsible shelf above a pool of water. There was a crowd of excited, laughing spectators standing around as the man in the dunk tank sang, "High and dry, Bobo doesn't lie. He'll laugh while you will cry and look the fool 'cause you can't put him in the pool." He exclaimed this signature phrase over and over again, along with other rhyming phrases, in a voice that sounded like a poorly played oboe, if an oboe could exude sarcasm. He'd pick people out of the crowd and incite them to pay "three balls for a dollar--get me wet or pout and holler."

He noticed a heavyset man walking by and yelled, "Hey, Mickey Lolich, come on up and show us how you won the 1968 World Series." The man's wife encouraged her husband and moved him toward the carny dispensing the baseballs. Although reluctant, the provoked man threw the three balls quickly, the heavy thuds of those balls hitting the tarp behind the target proving he wasn't, in fact, Mickey Lolich. The man waved his hands as if he were exasperated, but "all in good fun." Bobo sang his signature phrase and added, "Give up the donuts, Mickey my friend; then, come back and try again."

Craig was really getting into it. "This guy's great," he said. "See how he works the crowd? I could do this. I want to do this. He's like the fool in *King Lear*, remember? He could say anything to anybody without impunity."

"It's 'with impunity,' " I corrected. "Why don't you take a shot at it?"

"Why don't you, Geoff? You pitched in Little League."

"Yeah, Little League, impressive," I said as I accepted his challenge and paid for the three balls. When I stepped up to throw, Bobo sang, "Here's the hero come to remove Excalibur from the stone, untie the Gordian Knot, and slay Grendel." Bobo made me so nervous that the first ball fell short of the target plate, and the second ball went high. I wanted to throw the third ball right at Bobo, and in frustration I overthrew it hard into the ground.

I walked back to where Craig was standing, the crowd's humiliating laughter ringing in my ears, and said, "Let's go check out what else is here."

"Aw, Geoff, let's stick around. This guy's cool, and I need to learn from him."

"I thought you wanted to see the freak show."

"All right, let's go," he said, "but I am going to check out getting a gig like this."

"You know you'll get dunked sometimes."

"It's August, man, some punishment."

We walked the Midway, reacting to all the stimuli: the grinding noise of generators, the flash movements of the rides, the sounds of calliopes and music through loudspeakers. As we were walking, Craig kept howling "High and dry . . ." Then we heard the voice of the barker for the freak show. We paid four dollars each to enter what looked like an old trailer home with wooden stairs at the entrance and a dimly lit hallway with paneling on one side and windowed sections on the other. The first window had a sign that read "Tom Thumb, the two-foot man, is out to lunch."

"I think he's really in there, just too small to see," Craig said, drawing a laugh from the others in line. "Easiest gig in the world," Craig whispered to me.

The next window revealed "The Man with Two Faces," a stately looking man with a purple veil over the much enlarged left side of his face. He removed the veil to reveal a small mutated face with two nascent eyes, a small protuberance of a nose, and a slit of a mouth that worked spasmodically. There were barely audible gasps from some of the onlookers.

We then found ourselves looking through the glass at a girl about eight years old. There were ribbons in her hair, and she wore a cheerleader sweater and pink sneakers. A small third arm extended from her shoulder as she sat on a stool waving, a beautiful smile on her face.

We group of gawkers moved quickly and somberly out of the trailer and into the sunshine.

Craig was ahead of me and moving quickly. "What's next?" I asked him.

"I don't know. Let's get out of here and cruise Woodward for a while."

I agreed and as we climbed into the Mustang and left the fairgrounds, Craig seemed awfully subdued for the "class clown," a persona he usually displayed. To lighten the mood, I started chanting, "High and dry, Bobo doesn't lie." When he didn't answer right away, I said, "Hey, can I be there when you tell your parents that you want to be a dunk-tank clown when you grow up? I want to see their proud faces."

"Geoff, give me a break, will you? I can't get the image of that young girl out of my mind. She should be out having fun, not sitting there on display."

"I know. I wish we hadn't gone in there."

I had never seen Craig so low, nor had I ever seen him with wet eyes.

Flash prompt: Beyond the Sea

# Imagination Destination
## by T.A. Novak

When I timed the frothy waves lapping at the sand beneath my feet, they rolled in every three and a half seconds. The granules of Virginia Beach absorbed its tiny bubbles instantly.

Somewhere across the horizon, each wave began. Was it Spain or Portugal? Their slow, tired action told me they had labored the thirty-five hundred or so miles from a similar shore, from where didn't matter.

I wondered what it would be like to be over there at that precise point in time. Would I be at a beach similar to where I stood, teeming with hotels, luxury condos, surfboard rental shops, and restaurants, or would I be on the docks of a centuries-old fishing village, a place with no neon, no hustle and bustle, bobbing on the deck of a fishing trawler mending nets while the waves splashed against our dock's pilings?

These images conjured up thoughts of tranquility as the aroma of saltwater filled my senses, recalling the smells of Monterey, California, and those of Long Island, New York, places I had visited many years before.

I chose Portugal as the place where my waves began. That's the great thing about imagination; one could transport himself to a place like Salema, Portugal, a sleepy old fishing village with trawlers bobbing, waiting for high tide. There, a weathered old man began teaching a pale-skinned traveler almost as old how to mend nets and get ready to unfasten our lines and set sail for the deeper waters of the Atlantic.

Flash prompt: Drunk as a Skunk

## The Last Straw

by Mary Corrao

Small town folks know the crazy bastards that walk among them. As their police chief, so did I.

I was on my way home when I recognized the unmistakable rusted truck of Chance Ambrose, one of those crazy bastards. Pacing by the vehicle was Chance's stepdaughter Connie. I pulled up beside her and heard the hysteria in her voice. Chance's body slumped in the front seat reeking of alcohol. His head was bashed in. As usual whenever he was drunk, Connie had been called to pick him up.

Bruises covering Connie's face confirmed town gossip that Chance was a mean drunk. I spotted the bloody hammer in her hand. The weight of knowing what had happened hung in the air. The trouble with being a cop is you're always there after the fact. There are times in life when split decisions must be made. I made mine the minute I saw the battered girl waver as if a butterfly would cause her to fall. I caught her and placed her in my car then walked back to the truck.

I put the truck in gear, turned the wheels toward the one-hundred-foot drop, pushed the car over the edge then returned to the wide-eyed girl to cement our story. I laid out the false tale. Told her Chance had grabbed the steering wheel and she jumped out before the truck went over the cliff. In shock, I think she half believed it.

Lies and deceit never sat easily with me but glancing at the girl with her life ahead of her, my guilt slipped away. My body processed it like it was alcohol.

Some said it was a tragedy. Some called it murder. But they all agreed either way one crazy bastard was gone.

Flash Prompt: Drunk as a Skunk

## Wild Turkey, Double Shot
by Jane Schopen

"Larry, did you shoot us a turkey or a buzzard? This thing is so damned tough I can't cut it!"

Larry recognized the familiar slur in Sherry's speech. She was well on her way; hell, she was there. They both were. A steady flow of booze since noon had taken effect. First, the bottle of inferior bourbon gifted by his sister had to be suffered, then they cleansed their palates with the usual vodka lime.

"Gimme that and let me do it," Larry said, taking the knife from her hand. When several minutes of concerted sawing made barely a dent in the cooked bird, he could see that his wife had a point. Pissed off that she was right, he sawed harder.

"Jesus Christ!" Sherry growled, grabbing for the knife.

Larry held tight, and a short tug of war took place during which no kind words were exchanged. Sherry stopped struggling and stormed out of the kitchen. Larry chose a different knife and returned to the carcass with new resolve.

He had a funny premonition about his wife, about what she was getting up to. When he felt the hairs on the back of his neck snap to attention, he turned and saw Sherry pointing their twelve-gauge shotgun at his chest. As her trigger finger moved, Larry dove in, knocking the barrel upward.

The shot through the ceiling shocked, deafened, and sobered them. The gun clattered to the floor while they stared into one another's huge dark pupils.

Larry recovered the shotgun and shot the tough old bird.

# Heaven's Rainbow
## by Larry Quackenboss

"Daddy, will Momma see Grandma Lou when she gets to heaven?" Maddie, a precious four-year-old, asked her father as they leave the cemetery.

"Yes, Maddie, Grandma Lou will be holding open the gate for Momma," David Marston replied while holding back tears and remembering the night that his wife and Maddie's mother was taken from them.

In his mind, he could still see the delivery truck veer into their lane and hear the sound of metal on metal as the truck met his car a fraction of a second later. The truck hit the driver's side tearing off the front fender. David should have been driving, but he had been doing more than his share of celebrating the sale of his first book. With the advance money he received, he and his wife had gone to the little restaurant where they had first met.

"Will Grandma Lou and Momma hold the gate for everybody or just for Granddad Jon and you and me?" she asked, snuggling down and putting her blonde curls against his chest.

"I'm not sure how heaven works. It's been quite a while since I spoke to God," he replied.

"Momma and I said our prayers every night, and we always asked God to watch over you. Momma said you were going through some tough times. What are tough times?" Maddie asked.

David held his daughter just a little tighter while his tears dropped onto her curly locks. He did not know how he would ever be able to get through life caring for a four-year-old daughter. *What is going to happen to me? What is going to happen to us? I was barely functional when she was alive and could look after me.*

"Daddy, you're getting my head all wet," Maddie said. "Are you sad that Momma's gone to heaven? I'm sad, but I know she will be waiting for me to help her paint heaven's rainbow."

# I'm Hooked

by T.A. Novak

Guys need to have something to do to keep them out of the wife's hair. Some hit the bars; some play pool; some chase women (other than their wife), and some do dastardly things like fish. I fish.

I enjoy the sport of bass fishing. I do that in Michigan and try to in Lake Havasu. A friend of mine called and said, "Hey Tom. I'm bringing a boat I got at a yard sale. We won't have to go to the dock."

The fishing at the dock has been dead for two years. The invading mussels have taken over, eating what the shad used to come to the dock for. I was keenly interested in the boat. "How big?" I asked.

"Thirteen-six." Boats come twelve and fourteen feet, so it must be fourteen. But I didn't argue.

Two weeks later, Edie and I arrived at the house we rent, and the boat owner and his wife invited us for dinner the first night so that we didn't have to throw something together. That also gave me a chance to see the boat—the *Van Dam One*, as my friend named it. (Kevin Van Dam is a seven-time bass fishing champion from Michigan.) When we pulled off the blue tarp, I thought *Yep, definitely a yard-sale bargain.* It was old and dented with a cobweb or two under the seats and had a wood transom that was half rotted away. "Did you check it for leaks?" I asked.

"I figure we could put it in at Site Six some morning and find out. "He added that he had brought some good caulk that would fix any leaks.

"Is there a hose around the house?"

"In the garage."

"Let's fill it with water. If it leaks, you'll see where the water is coming from."

"Now why didn't I think of that?"

The first page of the *How to Fish* manual says, "One should never answer a loaded question put forth by a boat owner if one intends to fish from said boat." I did not answer.

I was hoping that filling it with water would also clean out the inside of the boat. It looked like it had taken in a lot of road dirt as it was trailered from Minnesota.

Yep, it had a few leaks, but the drips showed my friend where they were, and after draining the boat, he was able to patch them. The internal water dousing didn't improve the appearance of the *Van Dam One*, but I didn't expect much in something that was past due to go on social security. Yes, the boat was about that old.

A week later we launched at Site Six. Due to the size of the boat, I brought along a life jacket—just in case the caulk job wasn't all that good. I had dreams of fishing the surrounding shores as we tested the seaworthiness of our craft, but I failed to take into consideration that my partner is primarily a Minnesota Muskie fisherman.

A short explanation might be in order: My type of bass fishing is a slow, subtle working of soft plastic baits along a shore. Muskie fishing, on the other hand, is exactly the opposite. This fish, the Muskie, has the fisherman throwing very big lures, reeling it in fast, hoping to piss off the very big predator that the Muskellunge is known to be. The Muskie is the meanest freshwater fish in America. The record Muskie caught in Minnesota was a fifty-four pound, fifty-six inch fish. That's very big.

Our boat was a little crowded. In the front the captain had the gas tank for the outboard, a five-gallon bucket with an anchor, and about a hundred yards of rope. This meant I got the middle seat of what really is a rowboat and only about three feet from my friend, who as the captain, got the back seat and control of the motor.

"Where do you want to go?" he asked.

"Let's just work the shore."

The captain headed out to do just that. I started throwing a three-inch tube bait, something that mimics a crab, and crabs are in no rush while looking for whatever they eat. He started throwing something well over six inches with rattles inside and three treble hooks dangling from it. The boat rocked as he threw his big bait as far as he could and burned the water reeling it in. I was glad I had on the water-ski-type life jacket. I thought we'd be swimming soon. Surprisingly, I kept quiet. *He's the captain* I kept whispering to myself.

Twenty minutes later, whack. Two of the three treble hooks were impaled in the back of my life jacket. "Sorry, Tom," he kept saying as he worked to back the hooks out.

"Glad I'm wearing a flack-jacket. Why the hell are you throwing that big thing anyway?"

"Caught lots of fish with it," he said as he started rocking the boat with more casts.

Ten minutes later, WHOOSH! The big lure sailed within inches of my left ear. "Hey! Knock it off. You just missed my ear."

"Sorry," he said as he started casting with a side-arm move to keep the lure from hitting me.

Ten minutes and twenty casts later, WHAP! Something slapped me in the back of my head. "Oh Tom, I'm sorry," the captain moaned. When I moved my head, I could hear the B-Bs rattling within the lure.

"Sorry hell. How bad is it?"

"I don't know. I'm afraid to look."

"Cut the damn line and take me to shore."

"Why?"

"So a doctor can get the damn thing out."

Four hours later a stitch replaced the removed hook. Since then I've added some new equipment. A helmet. Fishing can be a dangerous sport.

# Running on Empty
## by Tim Montbriand

My family moved after I finished eleventh grade, and I entered a school full of strangers. When I walked through the doors of Lafayette High on the first day, a young man hurried to greet me. "Hi, I'm Robert Scales. Welcome to Lafayette." He was tall, had sandy brown, Kennedy-esque hair, and was impeccably neat. He looked like a model from a GQ cover. I learned later that his dad was a very rich auto dealer in town.

"Jamie Thompson, nice to meet you," I said.

"I know you're new here. If you have any questions, I can direct you to the right person."

I later found that he was telling the truth; he was a member or leader of almost all the school's clubs and social groups. After that first day, I would see him in the halls, and he would sing out a greeting and then dismiss me in a cordial but perfunctory way. He was always at the center of some group of students. He was popular, but I came to notice that he had no personal friends.

Bobby ran for President of Student Council that year, and the school administration, supposedly to instruct us on real-world politics, allowed the candidates to debate and answer questions from the student body. One other student was running for the presidency, Helen Rogers, a blossoming hippie. She spoke first:

"I'm going to make the administration let us decide what we should do with our student fees. We'll use that money for a grand carnival on the football field, with a live rock band and booths selling clothes, flowers, incense. We'll donate the money to a charity. We need to change the name of our sports teams from the 'Lancers,' those brutal horsemen with spears, to something less offensive. We will also get Ronnie back in school. He was unfairly expelled."

The student body cheered when Helen was done. Ronnie Wilson had been expelled when the gym teacher found a joint below Ronnie's locker—Now it was Bobby's turn:

"Thank you, Helen, I admire you for your strong beliefs, but we must remember that the student council already negotiates with the administration, and demands may be counter-productive. If I'm elected, I will show leadership in regards to those issues. I will seek common ground with the administration in regard to Ronnie's case."

When Bobby finished, there were no questions from the student body, and Bobby won at the ballot box the next day. I was stunned. Bobby's speech had been vacuous; he had offered nothing more than vague statements about "leading" and finding "common ground." Helen, at least, had concrete ideas and passion. I realized then why Bobby had no close friends. He had embarked on a higher mission, a political quest, and like religious clerics could not let anyone get too close.

Bobby came onto my radar about five years after we graduated. He was running for the U.S. House of Representatives after serving for a year in the Michigan State Senate. He had gotten a degree in political science—an oxymoron in my book—from MSU and was alleged to have wealthy supporters.

I was writing for the *Detroit Free Press* at the time, mostly obituaries and local social events, but when it was learned that I had gone to school with Scales, I was assigned to follow his campaign. I covered his speech to the Autoworkers Union. He assured his audience that machines would never replace humans on the assembly line. He had clearly upped his game since high school; he had mastered the techniques of misdirection and obfuscation. I confronted him about that deliberate vagueness during the press questioning following his speech. "Mr. Scales, you said that when you were elected you would lead the effort to form a committee to 'take a hard look at the issue of increased mechanization in the workplace.' What does it mean exactly to 'take a hard look' at a problem?' I envision a group of middle-aged men with furrowed eyebrows squinting at a poster that announces, 'Machines are putting people out of work.' "

"Thank you for that question," Bobby intoned as a teacher might answer a student's stupid question. "The fact of the matter is that there is no easy answer to that question. I believe in getting things done sooner rather than later. I went on an intense 'listening tour' to understand my constituents' concerns. At the end of the day, this is a critical issue that must be resolved, and we will stay laser-focused on and work toward that end moving forward."

I asked, "Mr. Scales, in your response just now you used four vague phrases to define the timing of your solution to the issue at hand. You stated, 'at the end of the day . . . this is a critical issue that must be resolved.' Do you mean the end of today, some other day? You must have meant today because that is 'sooner rather than later.' Also, wouldn't a 'laser focus' prevent you from seeing the big picture? And please tell me what you mean by the expression 'moving forward.' I know it sounds positive, but it is utterly meaningless. You could be 'moving forward' toward a cliff or certain doom."

Bobby was angry when he addressed me. "Why don't you stop criticizing my grammar and phrasing and focus on the issues. Look at my record, man. I co-sponsored a State Senate bill to ensure worker protections."

"You and all of the other senators," I pointed out. That's when Bobby's handlers gently removed me from the venue.

Bobby approached me outside. "What's the matter with you, man? Are you trying to sabotage my campaign?"

"You're an empty vessel, Bobby. Do you have any strongly held beliefs, or are you just trying not to offend anyone? If you want to be universally loved, learn to juggle and perform at kids' birthday parties. Or is it all about getting elected and gaining power?"

"You being in the media should know, Thompson. It's all about power. We're in the same game."

He had me there.

Flash prompt: Moonlight Madness

## Killing Time
by Mary Corrao

    Harry Time's death happened naturally—well not naturally natural, more like suddenly—leaving Silas with mixed feelings of relief and disappointment.

    Harry had long passed stocky, spreading to the area of morbidly obese. When Harry entered a room, his enormous size often made him an annoyance. But it was his enormous debt which made him Silas's target

    Silas, on the other hand, was slight of build and absent of color. He was the sort of man you never remember, an effect which served a hit man well.

    Though the two men were striking in their dissimilarities, both lived lives dangerously beyond society's norms.

    Silas first held a gun at the age of fourteen and thought it felt amazing. Although that feeling continued into adulthood ,he never killed out of hate or rage. When the time came to pull the trigger, he simply did it. It was merely business, and Harry Time was today's business.

    Harry wore a look of open-mouthed astonishment when Silas entered the room. For the first time, Silas felt a surge of sympathy for the massive man standing before him. His trigger finger lightened. And in that moment of hesitation, when life and death hung in the balance, Harry collapsed in a thud. Amazed, Silas stared at the lifeless body, which still held the expression of someone who was anticipating the worst. Next to him was the lethal weapon, a box of Krispy Creams, waiting to clog his already blocked arteries.

    Silas slowly made his inconspicuous exit from the building. He began to feel more like himself, which is to say he felt nothing at all.

Flash prompt: Moonlight Madness

## Magic Hands
### by Mary Corrao

Craziness lives in New Orleans, a profitable city for my talents. Preparing for a night of conquest, I dropped condoms in my purse and headed into the human jungle with a ready-for-trouble mindset.

The trouble came soon enough in the form of big brown eyes and a voice smooth as fine silk. His slightly disheveled look was just enough to be sexy.

"You look like a top-down kind of girl"; he smiled as he led me outside to a convertible Jag. We sped off, my hair blowing in the wind, our destination the yacht club.

"Divine vessel you own," I purred with admiration as we stepped aboard.

"Oh, it's not mine. Neither is the Jag."

We laughed out loud, abandoned our clothes, and engaged in titillating coupling on the deck of *someone's* yacht. His hands touched all the places where a girl loves to be touched while the moon cast a bright beam across our bodies.

*****

If not for the photograph of the man with the magic hands staring at me from the second page of the newspaper, I would have missed the accompanying article about the car thief picked up in a Jag. He wasn't as cute as I remembered, but the night before I had on brandy-fogged goggles.

A story on the opposite page about numerous jewel robberies alerted me. *Time to move to another town.* I lifted my coffee mug, the diamond bracelet shimmering in the light. My moonlight lover wasn't the only one with magic hands.

Flash Prompt: Moonlight Madness

## Let the Rumpus Begin
by Jane Schopen

I am alpha of this pack, and it feels great. I've got the experience and the chops. The juveniles stand about, fidgeting. They are magnificent animals with swift movements, shiny fur, and flashing canines. Above us, a glowing, golden orb casts just the right amount of light—and shadows. Tonight, we will move together.

The pack parts in deference as I stride to the front and position myself. Males and females separate to opposite sides of the arena. That is where it will happen: the gyrations, the couplings, and uncouplings.

All try to appear calm, but I know their restlessness of wanting. I see the surreptitious grooming and antics meant to attract one another. Pheromones permeate the air and snake through caverns of primitive young brains.

I make them wait.

When every eye is on me and the mass of bodies leans forward with expectation, I give my best wolf grin, turn to the orb, throw my head back, and emit a powerful, prolonged howl. The juveniles join in with an impressive array of shrill yips and wails that make my neck hairs bristle.

After the noise dies down, there is dead silence for a few seconds.

"Aaooooo, werewolves of London," I belt out.

Fellow band members join me onstage, and we explode into a contagious, stylized cover of that old song. Fast, driving rhythm gets the youngsters howling and hopping like Maasai jumpers. It's a promising start to the eighth grade "Moonlight Madness Fall Dance."

# The Letter
## by Larry Quackenboss

The soft, age-spotted, spidery hands took the bow off the box as they had done every Christmas for the last thirty-five years. She took out the brown-spotted and brittle letter and strained to read the words. It began as always:

My darling Lillian,

It's Christmas eve, and I'm writing this letter by candlelight. We hold the high ground for now. It's cold and damp, and it rains or snows almost every day. Half our force is sick, and it's my fear that many will not see the new year. I look down and see the enemy campfires below. They remind me of our town square's Christmas tree brightly lit. Those in command on both sides have declared a Christmas Day truce. In the sounds of the night, we sing a carol, and the boys on the other side reply. I've heard from my boys; they're trading with the boys in grey. We have a little coffee and trade for their cane sugar, something to make the Christmas spirit ring. In a day or two, we'll be back to the fighting; it makes no difference who is right or wrong. The killing just goes on.

Kiss the children and give them my love. I hope to spend my remaining Christmas holidays with you and them.

Your loving husband,

*Nichols*

On December 26, 1864, Lt. Nichols James Wamba of the Fifth Michigan Infantry was wounded and captured. He died in captivity. The letter was mailed by an unknown soldier.

# The Little Red School House
## by Larry Quackenboss

Johnny Naylor and his best friend, Harold Hopkins, sat on the creek bank fishing for whatever would hit the worm on the hook.

"So, Johnny, how's that schoolin' doin'? What's Ms. Ellen teachin'?" Harold wanted to know.

"She gave us a slate board and a piece of chalk, said we're gonna' learn how to read and write. She's gonna' teach us to write cursive words."

"Well, you oughta get an A cuz you know all those words," Harold said with a smile, showing his missing front teeth.

Monday morning came, and Johnny sat in the last seat of the last row next to the windows. This row held the kindergarten students.

Ms. Ellen came into the one-room schoolhouse and announced, "Today, we will test. I will start with kindergarten. Please come up to my desk to get a slate tablet and one piece of chalk."

The kindergarten class went to her desk and picked up the tablet and chalk. Ms. Ellen gave them the following instructions: "At the top of the slate, write your name and then write one word beginning with the letter D on the slate. When you are finished, please bring them to me."

Johnny wrote "Johnny Nash" in very clear cursive. He looked down at the blank slate trying to think of a cursive word beginning with D. The epiphany came upon him in a flash. The chalk screeched across the slate, and there was the word *Damn* in all its glory.

## Revenge Is a Dish Best Served Frozen
by Tim Montbriand

Leon Malosh waited twenty-five years to take revenge upon Gary Flinn for a beating Leon suffered at Gary's hands on the high school skating rink when they were both in ninth grade. Gary, a notorious bully, should have been in eleventh grade, but he had failed ninth grade twice.

Leon was bright, sarcastic, and witty. He nicknamed all the boys in class and was once heard to say, "You name someone; you own him." One of Leon's classmates told Leon, "Your first name spelled backward is 'Noel'; your last name's an anagram for 'Shalom.' Both words mean 'peace'; don't be so mean." No one knows if Gary ever heard Leon's nickname for him, the very unoriginal "Flunky Flinn," but many assumed that the uttered nickname had started the fight.

It wasn't much of a fight really. The guys had been skating around body checking each other in their heavy winter coats and thick woolen hats and gloves. The body checking escalated to fake slap fighting when Gary skated up to the group and slowly and deliberately pulled on his fur-lined, black gloves, like a knight dressing in armor or a gunslinger strapping on his six-gun. He whispered in Leon's ear, "Swing at me and I'll swing back. Swing at me again and I'll go down, make you look good." Leon then threw two ineffective slaps at Gary, who responded with several straight, brutal punches to Leon's face. Leon landed face down on the ice, the skates slicing the ice around him sounding in his ear like knife slashes.

Gary skated away smirking. The confrontation had been in fun, no one to blame, nothing to come of the event. Leon, on the other hand, felt humiliated as his face swelled and the bruising started, and he began to formulate in his mind an approach to settling the score. Days later, he would formulate a plan to avenge the wrong he had experienced and created the acronym **AVENGER** so that he wouldn't forget:

**A: Allow time to pass, the more the better, between the offense and the exacting of revenge.** Leon bought into the truth of the saying, "Revenge is a dish best served cold." The mistake many make is taking revenge too quickly when the antagonisms between victim and perpetrator are still fresh, and in the event of the perpetrator's demise, the victim becomes the immediate and likely suspect. Leon decided that he would wait twenty-five years. Who would link a murder to a twenty-five-year-old scuffle between two teenagers who'd had no interaction in the intervening years?

**V: Vilify the offender continually in your mind. Do not let a day pass without recalling the damage the offender has done to your life.** Leon had no problem with sustained vilification of Flinn. When Leon's father saw his swollen, bruised face, he said, "Who the hell did this to you?" Leon told his father that it was supposed to be a fake slap fight. His father said, "Damn, how could you let him do this to you? Stand up for yourself; be a man."

His father went to the school principal to complain, but the principal said, "Well, Leon is no saint and can sometimes say very provocative things." Leon felt the humiliating impotence his father must have felt in defending his son.

When Leon went back to school with his beaten pugilist face, the other students averted their gazes or tried to stifle their laughter. Gary, a heroic celebrity now, smirked non-stop.

After high school, Leon worked a series of entry-level jobs: pumping gas, working construction, cashiering at a convenience store, delivering pizzas. He had no drive to pursue a job more lucrative or prestigious. His self-esteem had been destroyed by Gary Flinn.

He was married for only a short while because his wife pressed him to be more ambitious and get a better job with greater pay and because he couldn't be honest with her about the obsession that drove him.

**E: Envision the many different forms of recompense you might employ in your revenge.** Initially Leon had envisioned killing Gary in a hit-and-run accident, or a drive-by shooting, but those acts would not allow Leon to experience Gary's suffering or see Gary's smirk disappear. What Leon enjoyed envisioning over and over again was tying Gary up and boxing his face so that Gary might experience the helplessness Leon had experienced.

**N: Never take anyone into your confidence concerning either the reason or the plan for revenge.** Even though Leon was somewhat sad about his failed marriage, he was very proud that he had never given anyone a clue as to the mission that obsessed him.

**G: Gather the gear necessary for each envisioned form of revenge.** Leon bought a taser, a gun, rope, and boxing gloves since his plan was to shock Gary into submission, beat the hell out of him, and then shoot him.

**E: Engage in espionage to locate the offender.**
The espionage was easy with the advent of Facebook. Once Leon was assured he could be anonymous, he discovered that Gary lived in Mt. Clemens, Michigan. He traveled there and bought the local paper, discovering that Mr. Flinn, the town's beloved police chief, had died from a rare form of cancer. His family had decided to put Mr. Flinn in cryopreservation in a facility in Clinton Township to be available for future medical research. The news enraged Leon.

**R: Remove the targeted individual from the living and revel in your success and bright future.** Leon researched the security flaws of the cryonic lab, and in the dead of night backed his pickup truck into the closed lab's loading dock, shut off the nitrogen to Gary's cryonic capsule, jimmied the seal, dragged the frozen body to the used freezer in the pickup, and drove to his garage. For years, Leon regularly defrosted the body and would either push Gary's facial muscles into a smirk or hang the body from the garage rafters and go all "Rocky Balboa" on it.

# Yard Work
## by Jim Veary

The phone rang six times before she picked it up.
"Hello?"
"Meez Hardy?"
"Yes."
"Meez Hardy, these ees Pug, the landscape man choo hire to fix your lawn."
"Oh yes, Pug. I am not home right now. I am on vacation with my family in Hawaii."
"Oh verry nice, Senora . That ezz verry verry good news. We have begun your lawn work as choo ask."
"That's fine, Pug, but I don't see . . . "
"Choo ask that we remove three trees and smooth out the lump in the meedle of the yard."
"That's fine, Pug, but . . . "
"We had a leetle problem, Senora."
"Oh?"
"You own a cat, Meez Hardy?"
"Yes I do. . ."
"A black cat?"
"Yes."
"A beeg fat black cat?"
"Well, Midnight is a bit overweight, but I wouldn't call him . . ."
"We tink the cat was hiding in a tree. No one saw him, but we all heard him when we pushed the branches through the wood chipper."
"Oh my God!"
"There was much black fur, so we tink he was a big black cat. We are so sorree for your loss, Senora."
"Oh dear, the children will be upset. But if that is all, Pug . . ."

"No, Senora, we had a leetle problem when we start to dig out the mound."

"Another problem?"

"Si. We find many, many bones."

"Bones? I don't understand."

"Beeg bones, leetle bones, many bones under the ground. My men they are afraid we dig up a cemetery, and they all walk off the job. They don't want bad Joo-Joo. I have no one to do the deegging but me and my cousin Raul."

"But the bones?"

"I feex, Senora. I rent exca. . . exca. . . a deegger machine and scoop them all up and shoot them through the wood chipper machine. Bingo-bango bones all gone."

"I'm not sure that was the right th —"

"Not to worry, Senora. They were probly not peeple bones anyway. They make nice mulch, but I spent money on the deeger machine and will have to charge you a leetle bit more."

"We can work that out when I get home, Pug."

"Si, Senora, but we had a leetle problem."

"Another problem, Pug?"

"The mound in your lawn was because of a beeg rock under the ground. We had to use the deegger to deeg all the way around eet."

"You tore up my lawn?"

"A leetle. But that was when we found the coffin."

"What did you say? Coffin?"

"Si, Meez Hardy, a coffin."

"A wooden coffin with a body inside?"

"Si. Is there anyone in your familee with red hair?"

"Oh my God! Did you call the police? You must call the police!"

"Oh no, no police. We deeg eet up and bingo-bango into the woodchipper. Eet is mulch with the old bones. All is good."

"Oh my God! I have to sit down. I'm going to faint."

"Meez Hardy, we had a leetle problem when we were deeging."

"Another problem, Pug? Now what?"

"Choo know choo have a beeg water main running under your yard?"

"No, I didn't know that."

"Choo do. We broke eet with the deegger machine."

"Oh my. . ."

"Much water came out and we had to call the city to turn eet off."

"How much water, Pug?"

"Veery much water. Eet washed a lot of dirt into the sinkhole."

"What sinkhole?"

"That was another leetle problem, Meez Hardy. The man from the city said there is a big cave under the ground, and the water was very great, and eet washed the dirt into the cave and made a big sinkhole. Eet keep getting beeger and beeger, and we couldn't stop eet."

"Oh my God!"

"Eet ate my deeger machine."

"I'm sorry for your digger machine, Pug, but what about my yard?"

"Oh your yard, Meez Hardy,. . ."

"What happened to my yard?"

"Senora, eet ate your yard also."

"How much of the yard, Pug?"

"The whole yard, Meez Hardy, di whole ting.""

"Oh dear God!"

"Eet ate your neighbor's swim pool, too."

"Stop! Stop! That's enough. Just let me go back to my family and make it through the last few days of my vacation."

"We had one last leetle problem, Senora."

"Don't tell me Pug. I can't handle any more."

"Si, Senora, but the policeman said to call you –"

"Policeman?"

"Si. He ask about the bones. I tink a neighbor call him, but not to worry Meez Hardy, my truck, eet fell into the sinkhole with all the bones, so you have no problem."

"Oh Dear God!"

"And anyway, dee policeman, he wanted me to tell you about the house."

"Pug? What about the house?"

"Senora, choo said no tell."

"TELL ME PUG!"

"I feel bad I ruin your vacation."

"Arghhhhh, JUST TELL ME!"

"Senora, the sinkhole, eet ate the house too. So I was wondering. . . where shood I send my bill?"

Flash prompt: Lost in Memories

# The Long Drive Home
## by Claudia Haeckel

Jordan made the long trip to visit Cecilia Marie twice a month. On his early morning three-hour trip to Sunny Horizons Nursing Home, Jordan was always hopeful. Being a religious man, he prayed for Cecilia to recognize him. Going home his thoughts roared and crashed in his head like the surf along the rocky beach in a storm.

Cecilia didn't recognize Jordon. Not once in the past four years had she known him. Every visit he had to tell her, "Hi, Cece, it's me Jordy. Remember when we got married?"

Today Cece laughed "You, aren't my Jordy! Jordy is much younger, not old like you. Where is Jordy? I need him to drive me home. My children need me."

"Tell me, is Jordy a good man?"

"Jordan is a very good man. He takes proper care of his family; he will do anything for his family."

"Cece, do you love him?"

"I have always loved Jordy. He makes me happy. He tells me I'm pretty and dances with me. The children love him; he always makes time for them. He plays the harmonica and can dance an Irish Jig. He can fix anything."

Cece sobbed, "What's happened to him? I know he would come and get me if he could. Something terrible must have happened for him to not be here."

"Oh, Cece, Jordy wants to be here with you. He loves you more than anything in this world. He thinks of you all the time. You'll be together soon."

# Lying Nights and Long-Neck Beers
## by Larry Quackenboss

It's true what they say about those redneck girls. There's nothin' quite so fine as one in tight fittin' jeans. I know they were spray-painted on cuz there wasn't a line or wrinkle showin'. There she was standin' at the bar just waitin' her turn. When she turned to watch the crowd, I noticed the front looked like my uncle's fifty Studebaker, great headlights.

I stopped lookin' after seeing the cold, sweaty long-neck beer bottle dangling from her hand. It was a Lonestar moment in my life. There before me stood a complete package. Once again, I was in love or lust; either way it was the real thing.

I shot her a look. "Ya'll wanna' dance?" I got the once over, and then came the answer, "Sure." She grabbed my empty hand and led me to the dance floor. It was quick, quick, slow, slow, the Texas Two-Step. We drank and danced right up to the last call. The more we drank, the slower the dance. The magical moment arrived. "Last call," shouted the bartender.

"How about I take you home?" I asked.

"How about a swim?" she replied. I grabbed a six-pack to go, and out the door we went. My pickup sat under the neon sign calling out "Bullit's 'n Beers."A quick kiss, two beers, and down the road to the Bender's quarry with Hank on the radio; it was just gonna get better.

Things were going well until a voice whispered in my ear, "I'll finish my surgical makeover next month."

# The Match
## by Tim Montbriand

Part 1

His trip along the Vegas Strip had been a blur of color and noise: fractured glimpses of shiny cars, reflective glass, shimmering pools, and bright garish lights—fluorescent, incandescent, neon. He had been hustled into the Mirage Casino past elevators, statuary, slot machines and down a flight of stairs into a small dressing room and was coaxed into a change of clothes. For the past few hours—last several days actually—he had been swept along by an ineluctable tide of events.

He was standing now in the boxing ring, not sure exactly how he had gotten there. The Events Center was full and raucous, and a noisy swelling tide had carried him past a phalanx of yammering, feral faces, had pushed him down the aisle to the ring apron and through the ring ropes. Someone pulled the silk robe from his shoulders, and he looked incredulously at the moniker there on the red silk—"Rocking Randy"—as if he hadn't seen it before. He bounced on the canvas a little; it was springy and made his fat midriff jostle. He stopped quickly, didn't know what to do. He looked down at the absurd sight of his hands in the bulbous red boxing gloves. He grabbed the top rope and leaned back, trying to ease some of the tension that stiffened his whole body. His whole professional life was now reduced to this one moment, and the embarrassment he felt was acutely physical.

Randy Shanahan was in a totally unaccustomed role. He was a disc jockey, a shock jock really, his fame built on controversial statements which had made him a celebrity but had also caused him trouble: his appearance this night, in this ring, in this ridiculous costume of red silk shorts and a wife-beater tee shirt that was too tight around his middle. He put the gloves to his face, as much to calm his quivering jaw as to strike something resembling a boxing posture.

Randy spotted Derek Vines, the WWMP radio station manager, in the front row ringside. Vines, ostensibly Randy's good friend and advisor, looked exultant as he talked to the woman beside him, a beauty with Vegas-showgirl flash and allure. Vines was short and slim with thin gray hair parted neatly above the thin fleshy face of a man in his late fifties, a stark contrast to Randy's own thick red hair and tall but corpulent frame at forty years old. Vines' heightened good humor this night of Randy's greatest humiliation bothered Randy in a way he couldn't quite formulate for himself in this moment.

\*\*\*

Derek Vines looked at the pathetic figure in the ring, "Rocking Randy," "Shanahan the Man," and was amused by—no ecstatic about—the big redhead's predicament. Randy had brought this night upon himself, telling the tough-talking female caller to his radio show two months before that no woman could ever beat up any healthy, normal man, insisting, as a case in point, that he himself could never be physically bested by any woman anywhere or anytime. Vines remembered the flood of calls from feminists that immediately followed. Their voices had been indignant, pinched with outrage. Randy had defended his statement, citing men's greater upper-body strength, their higher testosterone level, their more aggressive demeanor. His arguments only further enflamed the feminists—and the entire country it seemed from the volume of calls to WWMP—to insist upon a retraction of the statement or an agreement that Randy prove himself in the boxing ring against a woman. Randy was caught in a monkey trap.

So Vines had set up the match. He remembered now the look of entrapment, a kind of primal fear, in Randy's eyes when Vines had told him of the inevitability of Randy fighting a woman to silence his critics. Randy couldn't refuse; that would make him look cowardly. He couldn't win; that would make him a chauvinist bully. Beating up a woman would incite male champions for her honor, too, a fact that Randy himself had proclaimed as the basis, and only basis, for any female influence in the workplace.

Cindy Raines, a local fight promoter, called Vines, and he invited her to his sumptuous office at WWMP to discuss money. She showed up in sweatpants and a Champion sweatshirt, a knit watchcap pulled down over her ears. "I've got a fighter who'll kick Shanahan's ass," she said. She was confrontational, looking contemptuously at Vines as if she believed he were an advocate for Randy.

"I haven't spoken to Randy yet," Vines said, "but I don't see how he can avoid the match, given what he's said and all." He saw Raines soften a bit as she sensed that Vines agreed that Randy needed to be brought down a peg. "The only thing that might give him an out is the question of money."

"We'll cut him into a twenty-thousand-dollar purse and thirty percent of the gate. That's pretty good since he's a nobody. She's Taletha Green, undefeated in twenty-two fights. We think she's gonna be the best."

Any outcome was good for Vines. The station's ratings were through the roof, and the hype for the match would continue the popular interest. "I'll run that by him, see if he'll go for it, but he'll need time to do some training."

"No, no training. He shot his mouth off about how tough he was, how naturally stronger men are."

"I don't know. We don't want this thing to be the lopsided circus that the Bobby Riggs and Billie Jean King 'Battle of the Sexes' was."

"Riggs was an old flim-flammer, an ancient fart," Raines argued. "Shanahan's in his prime and claims he could whip any woman. He didn't care who she was. There's lots of women who can beat him. Taletha's sure to."

Vines agreed to the conditions and called to inform "Rockin' Randy" of the agreement. Randy, masking his secret fear, accepted the inevitable.

The day the fight was announced, the Mirage Events Center was sold out.

## Part 2

Randy felt the ring ropes tighten and the canvas heave, and he looked over at Taletha "The Avenger" Green and was shocked at her massive frame. She was fully six feet tall, only a bit shorter than he, and she was heavily muscled. She twirled her gloved hands and bounced effortlessly as if she were skipping rope. Randy felt the canvas bounce and, in sympathy with that movement, moved his own arms stiffly back and forth as he took a few bear-like steps from rope to rope.

***

Taletha looked at her opponent across the ring. She wasn't afraid of him, didn't feel any enmity toward him. The big man had a fat white midriff she would attack, puncturing it like inflated bread dough. This fight wasn't about brute strength; it was about timing, skill, dexterity. She had sparred with men before, felt their piston-like, hammering punches and was staggered but not subdued. She knew she could beat this man.

***

Randy started to relax a little bit and regain some of his normal confidence. He knew how he would spin the night's event. If he won, he would apologize for harming the poor woman, implying that her loss was due to the misplaced demands of strident feminists. If he lost, he would argue that he would have won a contest like no-holds-barred or mixed martial arts, contests in which he could use all of his innate, masculine strength.

***

Vines watched the two fighters as they were announced and was amused when the ring announcer boomed, "Taletha 'The Avenger' Green," exaggerating her nickname. She skipped to the center of the ring and bounced. "Rockin' Randy" walked limp-legged to the center of the ring and stood there shaking like a wet dog when his name was called.

Vines was happy to see the big prick totally humiliated. He looked around, satisfied with his own appearance at the vanity fair that was Las Vegas during televised events: businessmen in silk suits; hip hoppers with leather jackets, ostentatious jewelry, and lycra caps that looked like underwear; women like Vines' own date, candied fruit all dolled up in makeup, furs, nylon.

The crowd noise sounded like intense hive activity as the two fighters approached each other in the center of the ring. Vines had to laugh at Randy's tentative, mincing approach, his hand raised to block his face. Taletha moved purposefully, aggressively, and Randy took a step backward. Then, in a moment that came too suddenly, just as Vines was shifting to get comfortable viewing the fight, Taletha doubled Randy over with a hook to the belly and then knocked him to the canvas with a straight right hand. The crowd roared.

Randy staggered to his feet at the count of nine. As an over-eager Taletha charged in for the finish, Randy stumbled backward into the ropes and, according to Newton's Second Law of Motion, sprang back, striking Taletha in the temple with an extended lance-like arm. Taletha fell to the canvas momentarily stunned and attempted to rise, but her arms would not obey the temporarily defused part of her brain. She fell back to the canvas, grasping Randy's leg as he stood looking down in disbelief. She tried again to get up, but her balance was gone and she was counted out. For Vines, the image that stuck in his mind, the same one that would be on the front page of the sports section the next day, was of Taletha on one knee holding Shanahan's leg in a gesture of supplication.

***

Taletha remembered only being drawn into the curved space of the depressed canvas occupied by the fat man as a satellite might be drawn to the gravitational force of a large planet. Her eyes now were full of ripening tears that blurred her vision of the outrage all about her. Her corner men draped the robe over her shoulder and consoled her with comments like "It was a lucky punch" and "The count was too quick."

She thought only of her daughter, her grandmother, her promoter, and all the women who had supported her. She had let down her whole sex.

***

Vines groaned in disappointment over the outcome of the match, not only at the thought of a preening Shanahan, but also out of fear that Randy's braggadocio and unctuous comments about his victory might cause the radio station's ratings to drop. Busy playing out all of the complex ramifications of Taletha's loss, he wondered if the controversy that had generated so many listeners would evaporate? Would Vines have to get rid of Randy, his overbearing and supercilious cash cow?

The crowd was disappointed with the short bout, strident jeers rising above the murmuring din. Many were already yelling that the "fix" was in. Randy was booed and jeered as he made his way back to the dressing room. "Aren't you the tough guy!" one red-faced, heavyset man yelled.

"Come on. I'll beat yo ass!" a skinny little black man yelled. At first, Randy felt confident that, from his radio pulpit, he could sublimate what had happened in the ring and explain the anger of the men in the audience, but as the fervor around him intensified and the crowd pressed against him, he felt fear. Three security guards tried to escort him to safety, but they too were absorbed by the growing, pushing mob, which forced Randy out onto the street. Randy panicked seeing the mobs of men and women starting fires and throwing rocks while calling for Randy's red head for what he'd done to Taletha.

***

Vines stood up to leave after most of the other spectators were gone and took his date's arm, the balm of capitalist success soothing his social conscience. Maybe he would take his date to a fine restaurant for an expensive champagne and steak dinner before he took her to their rented room in the Mirage penthouse. Later, from his penthouse window, he saw the streets of Vegas aflame.

Flash prompt: Cupid Unrestrained

## One Can Only Try
by Karen VanderJagt

"I've had it. It's about time I interfered with what's going on down there." Cupid shook his head in despair as he watched. "They'll ruin everything."

"You can't always get the results you want, son." Venus tried to console her boy.

"Well, I may just take matters into my own hands." With that declaration, Cupid grabbed his special custom-made arrows and flew out of the temple.

Over the next week, Cupid shot arrow after arrow to try and achieve his grand scheme. After the last arrow hit its mark, he returned home and collapsed in exhaustion on the temple steps. Venus walked out and sat beside him. "Were you successful?" she asked.

"Let's see."

The two walked over to the great telescope the gods used for observing man and focused it on Cupid's targets.

Kamala Harris was having lunch with Ted Cruz.

Alexandria Ocasio-Cortez was playing tennis with Marco Rubio.

At a New Year gala, Donald Trump danced a waltz with Michelle Obama while Barack regaled Melania with tales of his childhood.

Mitch McConnell and Chuck Schumer laughed over a drink at a local bar.

"My, my, you have done very well," Venus said until she noticed one woman sitting by herself. "What about her?" she asked.

"I really tried to hit that Pelosi woman, but the arrows kept bouncing off."

# Moon Dance

by Jim Veary

The clouds boiled below me. Long arcs of lightning slithered between the towering curls like illuminated snakes, flooding the chaotic skyscape with flickers of shifting color. The clouds churned as far as I could see, flickering and menacing. On my left, a river of smooth air flowed between frothy mountains, looking like the Colorado River winding through the Grand Canyon. The comparison was imperfect as this river glowed aquamarine and showed rivulets of red swirls.

I had little time left before I plummeted down into those angry clouds. All my data was safe. I gazed up just as the moon slid past the horizon. This was not Earth's moon; it was Titan, the largest moon of Saturn slipping along on the outer ring of Saturn as if it were skating on golden ice. At over 5100 miles in diameter, it was bigger than the planet Mercury.

I waited for my last view of the dance.

Titan orbits well outside Saturn's ring system, glowing a pearly gold. I watched it slip higher in the black sky until another object entered my view. Tiny moon Enceladus zipped into sight, spewing a gossamer tail of water vapor from a volcano on its south pole. It ran just along the E-ring and quickly caught up to Titan. For the briefest of moments, tiny Enceladus eclipsed giant Titan. As it passed, Titan illuminated the spewing vapor cloud and painted it a shimmering gold.

Then my balloon was cut away. Rockets fired, and my pod swooped away from the mayhem and utter beauty of Saturn. The dance was over.

# Moonlight Kisses
## by T.A. Novak

The Marine Corps-issued mummy bag was zipped to my chin as I rolled over and glanced at my surroundings under a full moon. Gasping on its last breath of white gas, the mantle in the lantern on the nearby picnic table flickered. Playing cards were strewn about, some face up, some face down, right where the last hand of seven-card stud ended.

Ten fairly well inebriated card players snored; they, too, were in their sleeping bags that left only faces exposed. They were all finally asleep. I snickered, remembering what the Hawaiian, Johnny Abreu, had asked earlier. "There any grissless bears around here?"

Gunny Wynn, a black from Texas, quickly corrected Johnny, "It's grizzly bears, and no, there ain't any 'round here. Black bears maybe." Johnny stared nervously, checking over his shoulder as he played throughout the night.

We were at a primitive campground, enjoying two days away from our MP duties at Naval Air Station Moffet Field. This was a Marine Corps-provided, overnight party with all the steaks we could eat and booze we could put away for being the sharpest guard unit for the past three months.

I had the privilege to drive the two-and-a-half-ton US Navy truck carrying the sleeping bags, drinks, and all the food because I was the only one licensed to drive anything bigger than a pickup truck and happened to be a former charcoal broil chef at a restaurant named Stouffers in Detroit and, most importantly, was a teetotaler. The commanding officer, Colonel Dewey, appreciated my talents. I just wish I was a better poker player. I lost fifty bucks that night.

The lamp suddenly tumbled off the table, nudged by the first of four masked bandits munching on leftover Cheetos and chips. The bright moonlight illuminated scores more climbing over the Marines asleep on the ground. One paused to sniff the exposed face of Johnny Abreu, taking a lick of the whiskey residue on his lips. I chuckled again, remembering Johnny's island pronunciation for the "ra-coons." He didn't know a thirty pounder was now on his chest enjoying his Jim Beam-laced drool.

Moonbeams glistened off of the Hawaiian's face as in his sleep he smiled and pursed his lips, returning a dreamland kiss in the middle of the California High Sierra Mountains, circa 1960. "I love you too," Johnny murmured as he fumbled to cuddle with the ringtail. It fled into the night.

*Guess no more moonlight kisses for you, Johnny,* I said to myself as I dozed off.

# Not the Olden Days
## by Mary Carrao

"Once upon a time, there was a fairy princess."

"Grandpa, you don't say *fairy*. You say *gay*."

"I don't think she was very gay because she was being forced to wed the evil Black Prince."

"*African-American* is the proper term, Grandpa."

"He did not come from Africa or America. He came from a dark, evil land called Malefi . . . Do you have anything to add?"

"Nope, go on."

"Good! Her father was a good, kind man with one fault. He liked to gamble."

"You mean like Aunt Ethel does in Las Vegas?"

"Not quite. He made a bet with the evil prince, and the wager was his life. When her father lost, the princess offered herself in marriage to the evil prince to save her father from death."

"Why couldn't they just live together like my sister Amy and her boyfriend?"

"Because she had a better head on her shoulders than your sister."

"So, she was much prettier than Amy?"

"I did not say that! Let's just get back to the story. The only one who could save her was the honorable, handsome prince, but they had to get a message to him in time."

"Why not just text?"

"Texting did not exist in this faraway, enchanted land."

"*Enchanted* must mean olden days when they only had the first iPhone."

"*Enchanted* has nothing to do with iPhones. It means pleasant and charming."

"It can't be pleasant and charming if she could not contact the honorable, handsome Prince by texting and would have to marry the evil prince."

"I give up. Yes, they texted the honorable, handsome prince. He got in his super-fast jet pack, arrived in time to strike down the evil prince with his laser wand, and the gay princess and handsome prince lived happily ever after."

"But, Grandpa, if she were gay, she would want to live with a princess not a prince."

"Don't worry, my dear. It all worked out. Through surgery and hormones, the prince became a princess. One more thing."

"What, Grandpa?"

"Next time have your mother read your bedtime story."

# Politics

by Karen VanderJagt

This one lies; this one cheats.
This one's taxes are incomplete.
Words are said, true or not,
Seems the core has turned to rot.

Lose a vote then mob the streets
Not graciously accept defeat.
Courtesy has gone away.
Vicious words come into play.

Who is right? Who's to know?
Confusion only seems to grow.
Investigations all around,
Stomping truth into the ground.

Doesn't matter right or left,
All who care feel so bereft.
Disagree? Then shout them down.
No wonder truth begins to drown.

And journalism used to be
Exemplar of what makes us free.
Now they too have lost their way.
To whom I wonder do they pray.

Our America, to be just
Now needs leaders we can trust.
To work together for our good
And be the nation that we should.

# Portrait

## by Karen VanderJagt

Peter fell in love at first sight. She was beautiful, dressed in blue with a wide-brimmed hat. Her crystal blue eyes dulled the sky by comparison; her ebony hair reflected light. He wanted desperately to touch her skin because he knew it would feel like velvet. Her gaze was to the left as she looked out a train window. The soft light through the glass made her face look like porcelain; the blush on her cheek was like a rose. He knew her. To the depths of his soul, he knew her. Peter walked over to the portrait and glanced at the information on the card.

"Portrait"
Artist: unknown. Painted circa 1900.
On temporary loan from the Thomas Kline collection.

He took a seat in front of the portrait and spent the rest of the afternoon gazing at her.

Every day for the next month, Peter went to the exhibit during his lunch break. He would eat his pastrami and rye while he dreamed of the woman in blue. His conversations with her were silent because the guard at the doorway would have carted him away if he'd spoken out loud. He wondered what she was thinking. Was she pining for a lost love or dreaming of a love she'd yet to meet? He knew she was meant for him. She'd never be happy with anyone else.

"You really like that portrait, don't you?" asked a lilting voice. Peter looked up into the blue eyes of his love. "They tell me you're here every day to look at her. Why?"

"Because I know you . . . her. We were meant to be together. I know it makes no sense, and you might think I'm crazy, but that's how I feel."

"She was my grandmother's best friend. The story says she was waiting for someone, so she never married." The girl paused, then smiled a slow, sweet smile. "I sometimes have dreams where I'm wearing that dress and riding that train. So you see, I do understand."

"May I take you to dinner?" Peter blurted out. "Oh . . . I'm Peter." He felt like a fool.

"Hello, Peter." She smiled. "I'm Emily Kline, pleased to meet you." Emily stuck out her hand, and Peter took it. The moment their hands touched a current passed through them. *Finally,* they both thought.

When souls are meant to be together, they find a way . . . even if it takes lifetimes.

# Share the Road Rage
## by Tim Montbriand

    Mitch wheeled his Schwinn out of the garage, mounted it, and set off for work in the pre-dawn darkness. After he had gone a mile or so, he relaxed his grip on the handlebars, shifted his backpack, adjusted his sunglasses, and pushed his helmet up on his forehead. He realized that these little, oft-repeated actions were a great pleasure to him. He likened them to the reassuring, pre-batting rituals of his baseball heroes. He could hear the birds chattering as the sun began to rise and could sense a hint of petroleum lingering in the morning air.

    He rarely got tired on his bicycle rides, just really hungry, and he thought about the sandwiches he had in his pack and was pleased that he was early enough that he could stop at Mulligan's Café for a cup of coffee.

    He often became philosophical on his rides, and it occurred to him that he had missed so much in those years he had driven to work, shooting around insulated in a car, a mobile, metal isolation booth, in which he experienced neither nature's presence nor human interaction. He hated the expression "slow down and smell the roses" because to focus consciously on doing so would be to counteract the openness and spontaneity necessary to experience nature's gifts.

    Whenever anyone would ask him, Mitch would insist that he rode for transportation not for exercise. Cycling was now an integral part of his life, not some allocated segment of the day's activities. He was no self-conscious, posturing yuppie riding his bike in circles as part of some exercise regimen.

* * *

    As Mitch was rolling past his house, Hank was slapping at his alarm clock, which was set because he had been too tired the night before to print out the report he needed for his boss first thing this morning. He booted up the computer, thinking to open the file and start the printer before he dashed into the shower. The damned thing was so slow he banged the screen, and the computer rocked precariously on its side. His wife saw Hank's frustration and said, "Slow down and smell the roses, honey. You're too uptight. Why don't you stop at the gym on your way home and unwind on the stationary bike for a while before dinner."

"That's a good idea," Hank said. "I could stand to lose a few pounds."

When Hank came out of the shower, the printer was still laboring along. *Damn! I shoulda bought a faster laser printer.* When the document was ready, he ripped it off the printer, grabbed his briefcase and coat, slipped his tie over his head—he never undid the knot—and ran out the door.

At the McDonald's drive-through, he shouted his order and then squealed his tires as he was driving around to the pick-up window. He looked inside with a seething in his gut as the employees assembled his order. They seemed to be plodding around, talking and laughing. Finally he got his order and pulled out, driving with one hand while unwrapping his sandwich and trying to cradle his hot coffee with the other.

He'd burned his tongue on the hot coffee, and the Egg McMuffin was sitting heavy in his stomach when he saw Mitch ahead, halfway up the hill. *God these cyclists are a pain in the ass.* Hank couldn't slow down. He crossed the yellow line and accelerated.

\* \* \*

Mitch looked over his shoulder and picked up Hank's fast-approaching car. He extended his arm, signaling for Hank to slow down until he had crested the hill. Hank blew right by him, so close that he brushed the slack on the sleeve of Mitch's windbreaker, causing Mitch to veer off the road and slide on the loose gravel. There was no collision, but Hank's recklessness had triggered some instinctual rage in Mitch, and he cranked furiously downhill, catching up with Hank at the stoplight, hoping to drag him out of the car and kick his ass. With a sneer, Hank flipped Mitch the bird and sped off, denying Mitch even the satisfaction of an angry confrontation.

\* \* \*

As he drove along, Hank thought that if he'd had time, it would have been a pleasure to kick that punk cyclist's ass. He drove faster; he was going to make it to work on time. When he first began to hear a steady thumping, he figured the noise was caused by bumps in the road, but when he felt a heavy slag in the steering, he pulled into a strip mall parking lot with a flat tire. *Damn, I'm so late now I'm going to lose my job.*

As he was trying to break loose the lug nuts, Mitch rode up and said, "You ever heard of 'Share the Road'? You almost hit me back there."

"Yeah, I'll share the road when you pain-in-the-ass bikers start sharing the gas tax to maintain these roads."

"Why are you so angry? We don't cause damage to the roads. Can I give you a hand there?"

"Get me the spare out of the trunk!" Hank barked. "Here's the keys."

The cyclist wheeled the spare tire over to Hank and watched him fight the lug nuts while wiping the sweat off of his face and trying not to get his white shirt and tie dirty. Finally Hank attached the spare tire and threw the flat one into the trunk, which he slammed shut with a repressed rage. "Hey, bicycle boy, you should stay off these main roads; you're gonna get hurt bad someday," he said loudly. "Get outta here now."

"No, I think I'll wait for you to go first. I don't want you passing me again."

"I can wait," Hank said. "Hell, I've probably already lost my job."

Mitch rode down the road, relaxing again as he felt Hank's keys jingling in his pocket, but knowing he would have to find a new route to work.

# The Avenging Angel
## by Larry Quackenboss

Slowly the ornate wood door opened and the white-washed adobe walls reflected the sun, which shone through four small stained-glass windows. Rough-hewn pews showed the smoothness from years of wear. Red adobe tiles on the floor were smooth from parishioners walking to the front altar to receive the sacraments. The church was simple in its construction, but there seemed to be an aura within the walls.

Peter John Henry, or PJ as he was called, stood in the doorway removing his stained and dusty Mexican sombrero. The dark brown eyes took in the interior of the church. His face reflected the hot, dry, and windy land he had just crossed, yet he felt at peace standing in the entrance. PJ's body, hardened by years of working on the family ranch, relaxed, and a smile crossed his face, showing off his dimples and the twinkle in his eyes. *It is good to stand in the presence of a church* he thought. The small adobe church and the surrounding buildings had been home to PJ for two years while he studied and fulfilled his mother's wish to have one of her sons become a priest.

He knew he should first have a bath, shave, and get his shaggy blonde hair cut before entering such a holy place. His clothes could use the service of a laundry. His shirt had frayed cuffs and collar, and his jeans had patches. Scuffed and worn boots had more than a few holes in them. It looked like hard times were all he knew. But he knew God would not judge him by how he looked or the cut of his clothes. He stood ramrod straight walking into the foyer and down the aisle. The large Mexican style spurs with jingle bobs brushing against the stone floor echoed off the walls.

Carefully removing his gun belt, holster, and the .44 caliber Colt single action, he approached the altar. The gun and holster looked well cared for, unlike his clothing. After placing the gun and holster on the altar, he knelt down. The bright Arizona sunlight shone through the stained-glass windows, framing the gun and holster in a soft glow.

In a soft voice he began to pray, "Hear my plea, oh Lord, for it is forgiveness I ask for those things I have done and am about to do. Bless my gun and watch over me as I do my duty in your name. I am bound to bring all evildoers to meet their maker and dispatch them into hell, where they will be held until the day of redemption. May I carry out your will as an Avenging Angel?"

The priest, Father Garcia, stood quietly in the shadows until PJ rose, made the sign of the cross, and kissed the small cross hanging from the chain around his neck. The cross was a gift from his uncle Robert Porter of Boston. He took the gun and holster from the altar and buckled on the gun belt, tying it against his leg. Slapping his hat against the other leg, he watched the dust play in the sunlight coming through the windows.

With a soft cough, the priest came from the shadows into the light. Speaking in a quiet voice, he said. "Peter John, that is a very interesting prayer. But asking the Lord to bless such a weapon of destruction goes against His teachings. As His children, we are taught to follow His commandments, and they tell us not to take the life of another. As my former student studying for the priesthood, what do you know of weapons and the killing of men?"

"Father, I was taught at an early age the proper use of weapons. I am very good with a pistol and a rifle. Since leaving the church, I have practiced daily with both types of weapons.

My aim is true, and I believe I have been given holy dispensation to do what needs to be done. For the teachings in the Bible, Romans 12:19 states, 'Vengeance is mine; I will repay, saith the Lord.' It is vengeance that I seek for the killing of my brother," PJ replied.

"Son, it is the Lord's place to see that vengeance is carried out, not ours. I know you are versed in the scriptures, and you should know the next two verses speak of feeding and treating our enemies with kindness. Perhaps we need to discuss why you feel the call to do what you have set out to do. It is my duty as your priest and teacher to guide you in keeping your faith and help you find your path to follow," the old priest said.

PJ's shoulders sagged and his eyes blinked to hold back the tears that were forming. He realized his battle would be with the devil in trying to stay true to his faith. In a weary voice, he spoke of the reasons for his leaving the priesthood and taking up the trail of vengeance.

As PJ told the story, the words rushed from his lips. It was like a dam breaking, and with each word it felt as if a rock were lifted from his chest.

"Father, it's a very long and sad story," PJ said.

"I have time to hear your story and perhaps provide spiritual guidance to you," the priest replied.

"As you know, my family owns the Bar 7 ranch on the Arizona side of the border near the village of Naco. My father bid on and won an Army contract to supply beef and replacement horses to Fort Huachuca and Camp Rucker. It was the winning of the contract that started all our troubles. The original contract was held by a group of businessmen from Tombstone who lost it due to failure to meet delivery dates.

"Two months into the contract, just before we were to make our first delivery, a group of rough looking men rode up to the ranch. They introduced themselves as Tombstone livestock detectives looking for stolen and rebranded cattle. At the time, my mother and sister were the only ones at the ranch house. Mother said they were all armed to the teeth. The leader asked to speak to my father. My sister, Amanda, told him her father and her brothers were on the west mesa rounding up wild horses to break for the army. Mother said the men left and headed west toward the mesa.

"When my father and brothers returned with the horses, Mother told him about the men. He said they had not seen anyone up on the mesa. Father and my brothers caught fresh mounts and headed out to check on the cattle. He headed to the eastern side of the ranch; my brother Billy went towards the west, and Harley rode south towards the border.

"By evening, my father and Billy had returned and waited on the front porch for Harley. As the time grew late, they became concerned, and my father sent Billy to bed while he and my mother waited a little longer. About midnight they both went in and went to bed.

"At daybreak, my father rose and saddled a fresh horse, packed his saddle bags with supplies for a few days, and rode out looking for Harley. He found Harley's horse but no sign of Harley. However, about a hundred yards from the horse he found Harley on the ground dead. He'd been shot three times in the back. The men who shot my brother rustled a hundred head of steers. Those steers were to fill the first part of the Army contract.

"My father brought Harley back to the ranch and buried him the next day. After the burial, my father, Billy, and some of the neighbors went back to where Harley had been shot.

They tried to follow the tracks of the men and cattle. The trail led them into Mexico, but they lost the trail when the rustlers split the herd up.

"I was studying for the priesthood when this happened. I left, vowing to track down the men. With God's blessing, I will find the men who killed my brother and send them to hell."

"These men you seek, how will you find them? Do you know who they are?" the priest asked.

"My sister and mother said the leader carried his pistols in a sash tied around his waist, and one of the men had a special stirrup because he had a pegleg," PJ replied.

"What has become of your family? I understand your father has also passed," the priest said.

"My father was killed when he was thrown from a horse. My mother and brother Billy are working the ranch. Billy suffered a broken leg when he was younger. He fell out of a tree, and the leg never healed properly. He walks with a limp, but that doesn't stop him from being a top hand. If it can be done from a horse, Billy can do it. My sister's back in Boston living there. My mother's brother is Robert Porter, the archbishop for the Boston diocese, and she is staying with him," PJ said looking at the priest.

PJ could feel the emotions turning within his heart. There was a battle between what he felt he needed to do and what the priests at the seminary had taught him. It was as if he were had split in two with one side good and the other evil. He looked the old priest in the eyes and said, "I must do what I have started out to do."

Turning, PJ started back up the aisle to the door. As he reached the door, the priest called out to him, "I know you know the difference between good and evil. You were taught what is expected of a man of the cloth. The fight you are having in your heart and soul is good versus evil, and you do not want evil to win. Should you like to spend some time with me, perhaps we would be able mend your heart and allow the sun to shine into your life. You are now filled with hate, and hate for your fellow man is an evil thing. If you are set on leaving on this vendetta, would you allow me to hear your confession, my son?"

"No, Father, my confession will be heard when I finish the job I've set out to do. Then the good Lord can absolve me of my sins," PJ said, walking out into the bright sunlight.

The leopard Appaloosa stallion stood waiting at the hitching rail. Grabbing the reins, PJ swung into the saddle and headed towards the town of Miller Crossing. As he left, he heard the priest say, "Vaya Con Dios. I'll pray for your soul."

Flash prompt: Feel This

## Some Things Gone with the Wind
### by Tim Montbriand

There had been a red sky the night before, so he headed to the marina. He walked the shaky dock of the marina to his sailboat, the "Moon Fixer." He stowed the sail covers in the cabin, dropped the rudder, and bent to start the outboard. He uttered his usual incantation, masking his utter contempt for the internal combustion engine: "C'mon, sweetheart, be good to me."

He made it out past the breakwater and distanced himself from the rumbling of the power boats and the irritating mosquito whine of the jet skis. He shut off the engine and raised the sails, felt the power of the wind through the tiller, braced himself against the boat's heeling, and experienced his longed-for escape from the noisy, mechanical world.

As the zephyr wind pushed the boat, he relaxed and watched the beauties of the coastline pass by him. He gained open waters, reveling in this world devoid of tedium and stress. He never tired of watching, through the billowing sails, the bow bobbing on the cresting waves and kicking up spray.

Later, he'd sail back to the marina through the channel; the wind was aligned perfectly. Usually, when he had motored through the channel and observed the antics of the natives, he felt as Marlowe must have felt traveling through the "Heart of Darkness"—"Oh the horror!" Today, though, he saw the frantic bodies leaping to the heavy pulse of the music and, like Kurtz, thought it might be fun to join in.

Flash prompt: A Blank Slate

# Time to Move On
## by Mary Corrao

Tex flashed a smile that displayed his teeth, all four of them. "Of course, it involves a woman. All the best stories do."

The bartender, his stomach bursting past his suspenders, laid beer in front of the grizzled old man and the young cowboy. Tex raised his glass, chugged it down, and leaned in toward the young man.

She was a blonde, slender thing with sassy eyes. When she fixed those eyes on me, I fell in love. I was a good-lookin' buckaroo back then."

The cowboy searched the old man's face trying to find the young man he must have once been.

"Her talents were varied if you know what I mean." Tex winked and flashed a smile. "I was startin' ta plan settlin' down with her, sittin' by the fire, she cuddlin' up against me, and me playin' my harmonica. Then she says, 'I'll miss you when you leave tomorrow.' 'Leave?' I says. 'I thought we had somethin' special.'"

"Oh, it's special. It's called adultery. My husband returns tomorrow."

"I let the words rattle around in my head while she placed her lips on mine, just enough to make me want more but . . ."

"But what? What did you do?" the wide-eyed cowboy anxiously asked.

"Do? Why I put on my britches, headed out the door, and started my life roamin' the range. Remember this, son, there's a time to move on, a time to stop lookin' back, and a time to start with a clean slate." Then he raised his glass again, reached into his pocket with his other hand, and pulled out a small metal object. "But I still got that harmonica."

Flash Prompt: Sexy Siren

## Taking the Bait

by Jane Schopen

After an extended coyote chase, Maureen's dog Wyatt returned to her, panting and exhausted. The big golden retriever never moved gracefully, but now he looked downright drunk as he stumbled and half-dragged his hindquarters. When he collapsed at her feet, she tugged him to the scant shade of a palo verde tree and doused him with water.

Maureen knew the risks of walking her dog off-leash in the hot desert. She was angry with the coyote—and herself. The animal had appeared at the start of the hike and began a provocative, shrill yipping. Wyatt obeyed orders to stay at her side until the coyote's taunts proved too great.

"Was she worth the trouble, lover boy?" Maureen chided Wyatt while stroking his wet, brush-laden fur. "Did she take you to meet her folks?"

The heaving dog couldn't drink, much less walk. Maureen wondered how to get him back to the jeep before it got even hotter. Looking around to formulate a plan, she saw the same pesky coyote nearby, watching.

*I could shoot it.* The idea popped into her head so suddenly it dumbfounded her. Maureen rarely gave a thought to the Glock strapped at her right hip, a gift from her husband who worried when she hiked alone. She had learned to shoot and carried it—mostly to appease him—but still felt ambivalent about the weapon.

The coyote didn't threaten her. She was irritated by the stalking. Surprised at herself, Maureen drew the gun, took aim, and zinged one above the animal's head.

## Prick of the Needle
### by Karen VanderJagt

    Murder for hire is a lucrative business especially when you're as good as I am. I'd just turned thirteen when circumstances made me realize my talents. Now I'm an established professional and can pick and choose my clients. And as all good professionals do, I know my specialty.

    Barry Goodman, who really wasn't very good, was next on my list. My costume was perfect, just the right mix of naughty and nice. I sat all prim and proper on the park bench where Barry was expecting me. His long black limo drove up and paused in front of me. When the back door opened, a plump ringed hand reached out towards me, so tossing my long blonde ponytail, I stood and approached with a sweet innocent smile. I placed my hand in his, and he pulled me into the lush black leather interior. I could smell his aftershave, way too heavy for my taste, but I've noticed that tendency in my specialty.

    "Let's take a nice long drive," Barry said to his driver over the intercom." Would you like some champagne?" Barry asked, patting his lap.

    "I'm not old enough to drink," I simpered.

    "Just this once," Barry coaxed as I straddled his lap and reached up to pull out the stylus that held my hair up. Barry seemed mesmerized as the golden locks cascaded down my shoulders.

    Barry sighed and smiled a very satisfied smile. He was happy with his choice and was pouring my glass of champagne when the eight-inch, sharpened stylus pierced his heart. His final look was one of surprise.

    "It's done," I said over the intercom extracting the needle and wiping it clean.

    The chauffeur executed a U-turn and drove back to the park, lowered the window, and handed me an envelope of cash. "He was eyeing my little sister," he said glaring at Barry with disgust. "We thank you."

"You're welcome." I got out of the limo and walked back into the bushes where my bag waited. Taking off my working clothes and the blonde wig, I got dressed and headed for home. I still had homework to do, and Mom would shoot me if I was out past curfew.

Flash prompt: Lost in Space

## Space Junket
### by Tim Montbriand

It had been twenty years since *Blue Origin* (Bezos' Bomb) and the *Virgin Galactic* had initiated recreational space travel for wealthy tourists, and Brice Paulas wanted in. He was eighty-three years old, wealthy, and insatiably curious. Most of his friends were either deceased or living in assisted living facilities, but he still felt vigorous. He booked passage on the *Sweet Orbiter*, a spaceship that traveled sixty-two miles to the edge of space and orbited the earth in twelve hours.

As he strapped himself in for takeoff along with the other passengers, he felt a bit nervous, but when the tremendous thrust of the engines pinning him to his seat eased, he felt great relief, realizing what an anchor earth's gravity was to the freedom of the human soul. When the *Sweet Orbiter* eased into orbit, Brice and the other five passengers floated weightlessly, giggling and assuming physical positions impossible for them on earth.

"Now it's show time, folks," the cruise director shouted. He gave each of the passengers a space suit and led them up a short stairway and out a hatch that revealed a six-poled carousel above the ship, to which he tethered each adventurer.

Brice was ecstatic as he went slowly in circles, awed by the blue-green marble of the distant earth, so delicately vulnerable, and for the first time, he felt a visceral understanding of infinity. He was pulled from his reverie by a heavy impact that shredded his tether and caused the side of the ship to crumple.

"Captain," the first mate cried. "We've been hit, and one of the passengers, Brice Paulas, is now on a fast trajectory away from the ship."

"Damn all this space junk! Crap floatin' everywhere. All that money and material lost. Okay, have the engineers pull a drone from the bin and send another tether to Mr. Paulas."

Moments later, the captain heard the repeated message "Danger Will Robinson."

"Who the hell's screwing around down there? Communications are to be scrambled to protect company procedures."

"That message is scrambled, Captain," the first mate insisted. "The unscrambled message is 'Drone bin is all wrong.' The space junk hit the bin and they can't send the drone."

"Well then, radio Mr. Paulas that we'll find a way to retrieve him."

"We did, sir, and he replied, 'Don't bother.' "

Flash Prompt: Knowing When To Run

## Stand Your Ground
by Mary Carrao

Alexander Maestreda was kicked out of school in the fifth grade. Everyone speculated on the unspeakable reason he was expelled. Because it was unspeakable, no one spoke of it, and no one actually knew.

The mystery added to Alexander's allure. Combined with his gorgeous looks and don't-give-a-rat's-ass attitude, it made Alexander deliciously irresistible.

My girlfriends and I purposely strolled by his house one afternoon in June delighted to find him out front, stick in hand, poking at worms. A hard rain the night before had brought the fattest, bloodiest, slimiest creatures to the surface.

As we gathered around our heartthrob, my friends were sucked into helpless adoration. But I noticed a mischievous glint in those big brown eyes and a slow smile just before a flip of his stick landed a bloodsucker smack in Rosemarie Lamicella's hair. Several more flying worms sent my screaming friends running while I stood my ground, knowing that wild things always give chase to anything that runs.

Just the two of us were left. He turned his attention from the worms to me. And that's how I was launched into the most exciting, adventuress summer with Alexander the Great.

He moved away that September, but until then, jealousy dripped from my friends' lips when they asked, "Why is he always with you?" With a mischievous glint in my eye and a slow smile, I answered, "You've got to know when to run."

# Call a Marine
by Jim Veary

# Chapter 1

Charlie Rizzo has been my best friend since kindergarten. Our friendship was bonded when I saved him from a vicious assault by the class bully, a five-year-old girl named Mindy. Charlie was short and chubby back then, and the butt of youthful verbal abuse. Mindy was merciless, dancing around him chanting a "Charlie is fat" song of her own creation. The other kids just stood around and laughed until I stepped in and pushed her down in the sandbox—a bold move for a scrawny five-year-old.

She cried. The laughter stopped then started again, only this time they were laughing at Mindy. Charlie beamed and vowed to return the favor some day. He has never stopped returning the favor.

By the time we reached high school, he was no longer Charlie. We called him Rizzo, and he had built himself up to be the all-state defensive tackle on our football team. He was still short at only five-two, but all that fat had gone into muscle. I was a mediocre pitcher on the school's baseball team, and he took to calling me "Hardball."

Everyone knew Rizzo and Hardball were inseparable friends. We were an odd couple. Rizzo was Italian, swarthy, and hard as granite. He had a face that looked like it had been squashed in a hydraulic press, but he had a smile that split that face in two and lit up a room. I was the Irish boy, white as snow, six feet tall, and willowy. Compared to Rizzo, I was a chick magnet.

We graduated from high school with no idea of what we wanted to do with our lives. Rather than face the draft, we enlisted. I chose the Air Force with visions of the wild blue yonder but ended up an aircraft mechanic and never did get off the ground until the last year of enlistment when I shipped out to Ton Sun Nhut airbase in Vietnam. I would have happily passed on that flight—on that whole last year as a matter of fact.

Rizzo, of course, would have none of that sissy Air Force. He enlisted in the Marines. Rizzo wasn't much for writing, so our letters back and forth were meager. I never knew where he was at any given moment, nor did he seem anxious to tell. But we stayed in contact, or so I thought.

It was October 1972 and Henry Kissinger had said, "Peace is at hand." C-130's and C-5A's were making daily flights filled with troops returning home. Our combat footprint was dwindling. I didn't know it at the time, but the last soldier would leave Vietnam five months later in March of 1973, and it was all for naught as Saigon fell in April of 1975. But what I did know is that we were still taking mortar rounds over the outer perimeter, and we were still shipping out casualties and body bags on the medical flights back to the states. If this was peace, I would hate to see war.

My assignment for those final weeks in country was to assist the loadmaster in getting departing troops settled aboard their aircraft. Most of that work was happy work. The guys were going home, and they were excited and boisterous, having a real hard time maintaining military discipline. But even the happy faces carried a pallor to them, a coating of wary intensity that war manages to apply in ever-thickening layers. There was an air of relief, but it was mixed with a sense of anxiety to get the hell off the ground before something bad happened. Something bad was always happening in Vietnam.

It was the medical flights that tore at your guts and left you dehydrated from the tears you tried to hide. These men were broken in ways you couldn't believe a human body could break. They were missing limbs and eyes and even faces, their punctured bodies swathed in bandages and smelling of iodine and blood. They were all going back to the states, with a stop at Ramstein Air Force Base in Germany for the casualties that might not make it all the way home.

I was sitting on the loading ramp in the nose of a C-5A when the first of a short caravan of ambulances pulled up. There were ten ambulances assigned to the Evac. Squadron. Six were lining up while others staged at the edge of the apron. It was time to go to work.

The first ambulances carried caskets, and I helped the medics carry them to the rear of the aircraft, where they would remain hidden from the living breathing patients to follow. Only six caskets this trip. That was good news for everyone except the guys inside the boxes. Once the caskets were unloaded and shrouded in the aircraft, each ambulance returned to the staging area to take on the injured G.I.'s.

A steady stream of ambulances approached the aircraft, and we helped the walking wounded to their seats. The C-5A was the biggest cargo aircraft in the military arsenal. It wasn't your typical 707, not something you would expect to be flying on TWA. Seating was minimalist and hard on the arse, and the interior was cavernous, noisy, and drafty when in flight. The seats were arranged along the sides, leaving the centerline of the plane for the stretchers.

Once we had the walking wounded belted in, we switched our attention to the broken men in the stretchers. Military doctors and nurses accompanied the wounded, keeping close check on vitals as we locked each stretcher into the floor tie downs. Most of the guys were heavily sedated, but a few were alert. There was a soft murmur of voices as we got everyone in and settled.

We finished up and I stood in the open doorway and saluted all those brave guys. Then, as I turned to leave, I heard a whispered voice float out of the murmur. "Hardball?"

I turned on my heel and peered back into the aircraft. Only one person would call me Hardball. Three rows down the aisle lay a figure swathed in bandages. His face was unrecognizable beneath the shroud of white cotton, with only his eyes and a slit over his mouth and nose exposed. But his eyes were still the same intense blue that I knew so well. Rizzo!

I moved toward him, trying not to run.

"Hardball," he whispered again, and there was no doubt left. Pinned to the bandages, was a Silver Star with a Purple Heart beside it.

His right hand twitched in greeting, but the arm that once held his left hand was completely gone. The guy had been through hell.

"Rizzo, Jesus Christ!"

The flight crew was walking down the length of the aircraft making last minute checks while the engine started to whine as they were spooling up to military power. "Ya gotta get outta here, airman. We're closing up."

I nodded. "Rizzo, I gotta go. But I'll find you wherever you are, and I'll be there for you."

"I'm depending on it," he muttered through clenched lips.

I turned and marched down the ramp, tears welling up in my eyes. That last glance at Rizzo had shown me something extraordinary. Tears pooled in the bandages edging his eyes, wetting the cloth. It was the one and only time I ever saw Rizzo cry.

## Chapter 2

Two weeks later I was aboard my own C-5A en route to the states. I learned through channels that Rizzo had gone directly to Walter Reed Hospital in Washington. I also learned what that Silver Star was for.

Rizzo's platoon had been assigned an interdiction patrol in Quang Tin province, just south of Hue. They were ambushed by a company-sized force of NVA regulars and only survived with the help of close-in air support and a C-130 gunship. The evacuation Hueys started arriving fifteen minutes after the engagement began, but the jungle was thick at the platoon's position, and they had to use a narrow clearing that only accommodated one helicopter at a time. Each UH-1 Huey held twelve men. A Marine platoon is composed of forty-two men. The math was simple. The evacuation would take more time than they had.

The four men composing the heavy weapons unit were ordered to protect the rear, and the platoon started evacuating to the chopper landing zone. Rizzo was in charge of the M-60 machine gun, nicknamed "the Pig," because the weapon weighed twenty-four pounds, plus ammo belts carried by a second man. It was a beast to carry through the jungle, but the M-60 could huff and puff and blow a house down.

The retreat was orderly. Rizzo and the other M-60 gunner set their weapons on bipods atop a fallen tree then raked the jungle around them. They paused, waited for return fire then concentrated their fire on those points. Without speaking, they grabbed their weapons and sprinted twenty yards toward the landing zone then dropped, set up once again, and repeated the scathing fire.

The enemy followed them, drawing closer with each stop. Rizzo could hear the landing choppers, but so could the enemy, who redoubled their efforts to overrun the back-door team.

They finally broke into the open and used the last of their belt ammo in a vicious sweep of the jungle. The return fire was blistering, and Rizzo's beltman went down with a shot in his chest. Dropping his smoking gun, Rizzo scooped the man up and carried him to the last chopper right on the heels of the other M-60 team. They all tumbled into the back of the chopper, which immediately lifted off the ground. A corpsman moved to help the wounded man, and Rizzo stood to get out of the way when a loud clank drew his attention to a rocket-propelled grenade smoking on the deck. He picked it up without hesitation and tossed it out the door. It exploded before it had gone three feet, shredding his arm, filling him with hot shrapnel, and blowing him back into the chopper. He survived, but thanks to his singular act of heroism, so did the aircraft and the nine men aboard. Thus, the Silver Star and the Purple Heart emblazoned his bandage-wrapped chest.

Surgeons at the 45$^{th}$ surgical hospital in Tay Ninh had no choice but to amputate Rizzo's left arm and spent many hours removing what they could of the shrapnel throughout his torso. However, he needed more extensive care than they could give him in the field. The decision was made to air-evacuate him to Ton Sun Nhut air base, where I finally encountered him in that C-5A. My friend was a hero, but he had only narrowly avoided being a dead hero. I couldn't get back to the states quickly enough.

# Chapter 3

"Charles Rizzo?" I inquired at the nurses' desk on the third floor of the Walter Reed National Military Medical Center. I was in civvies, having received my honorable discharge once I set foot on American soil. My one and only task was to book an immediate flight to Washington DC.

"315," she said, pointing down the immaculate hallway before returning to her clipboard and charts.

I aimed an unseen nod her way and moved down the hallway until I saw Room 315. The door was ajar, and I pushed my way in. Rizzo was sitting up in the single bed looking a lot better than he had two weeks earlier. He still had more bandages than skin; his face was puffy and swollen, but his eyes were bright and alert. He looked my way and scowled. "Took ya long enough to get here," he said and grimaced. But the smile was already developing at the corners of his mouth.

"The Air Force doesn't move as quickly as you, buddy."

"Pussies," he responded.

"Yeah. Maybe," I said, then strode to his bedside, leaned in and hugged him. "God! It's good to see you."

"Same here, my friend." The smile was spread across his face by then, maybe the first smile he'd had since Quang Tin.

# Chapter 4

It took two years of therapy and surgery to get Rizzo back to being Rizzo again. He got a medical discharge and a job counseling amputees in the V.A. hospital in Phoenix. I followed him and landed a job as a mechanic at Sky Harbor airport. Life went back to normal, including our regular visits to the local watering hole.

I walked in, looking for Rizzo and had the exquisite good luck to find a barstool next to the prettiest woman in the place. Beautiful women tend to intimidate a lot of men, but not me. I'm attracted like iron filings around a magnet. I sat down, ordered a bourbon on the rocks, and started a pleasant conversation that was taking its own sweet time, but going nowhere. That's quite alright, because I had nowhere to go and the rest of my life to get there.

We had almost reached the point where an exchange of names seemed appropriate when a pack of buffoons swaggered into the bar. I saw them in my peripheral vision and knew they would be trouble for someone. It turned out that someone would be me.

The Alpha mutt was tall and looked like he stuffed his shirt with old socks—muscle mumps everywhere. He scanned the bar until his eyes found the blonde I was chatting with. He smiled and strode up to us and slid between the two barstools, ordering three beers from the bartender. "Hey," I shouted. He turned and glared at me then turned to my "almost date" and leaned in to talk to her. She scowled and wrinkled her nose at the smell of his breath.

"Hey, asshole! Move it."

He turned and slammed his open palm into my chest, knocking me right off the stool and onto the floor. "Who you callin' an asshole?"

The bar got suddenly quiet. I heard the stool behind me push back. "Uh Oh," I thought.

Rizzo reached down and helped me to my feet then focused on the Alpha. "You need to apologize to my friend and leave that girl alone," he said in a voice that was almost cordial.

The Alpha turned and looked Rizzo up and down, noticing the one sleeve pinned up to the shoulder. He snickered and said," And you're gonna make me?"

"If need be," Rizzo answered. "Somebody's gotta teach you some manners."

The Alpha snickered at his two buddies and turned back to Rizzo. "A one-armed midget is gonna teach me manners? I don't think so. Go back to Oz, Pal."

Rizzo leaned in and lowered his voice. "Mister, you've got one opportunity to change the path you're on. You can walk out that front door and wake up in your own bed tomorrow morning, or we can go out that back door and you'll wake up in a hospital bed in a world of hurt."

"You and your scrawny buddy gonna take on all three of us? Really?" He moved toward the back door. "Come on, guys. This is gonna be fun."

"Rizzo," I called out, "Don't kill em."

He smiled and replied, "The little guy in the back, you hold onto him. I'll take care of the other two."

We all walked out the back into the cool night air. A few of the bar patrons followed us. I looked back and saw my "almost date" watching with interest from her stool. Behind her, the bartender was on the phone. We didn't have a lot of time for this.

Rizzo faced off with the big Alpha. The other two buffoons took positions to Rizzo's left and right. The big guy showed no fear. He should have.

Rizzo is the most awesome warrior I have ever seen. He learned every trick the Marines could teach him and a few more that the enemy accidently taught him. He didn't look like much, but he was a fearsome fighter.

The Alpha should have been very fearful. Instead, he stood there trash talking, working himself up to throw one huge punch. Rizzo knew all the tells, all the little things that signal a coming punch. When the Alpha moved his clenched fist backward just a bit, Rizzo shifted his weight to his toes and was ready when the punch came. He leaned back and the sudden swing missed his jaw by a half inch. Just as it flew past him, Rizzo leaned forward and leaped at the hulking brute in front of him, his right arm acting like a piston and driving his fist into the man's face. I heard bones crack and shatter, and the Alpha went down.

Rizzo kept the momentum going and pivoted on one foot, bringing the other foot up into the chest of the second buffoon. The breath went out of the man in a whoosh, and he collapsed to the ground gasping in a frantic attempt to get air.

Buffoon number three was having no part of this and turned to run. I grabbed him and wiggled my finger in his face. "Uh-uh. Stick around a bit." At last someone was afraid.

The fight was over before it even began. Rizzo checked them both to make sure they were still alive then brought his right boot down on the Alpha's open right hand. I heard more bones shatter, but the guy didn't stir.

We walked the survivor back into the bar. The jukebox was blaring a Toby Keith song –

> Call a Marine
> Instead of 911
> They're built to improvise, adapt and overcome
> When you're in knee deep and you're up shit's creek
> And you've tried everything
> Tell you what you do
> Call a Marine!

It seemed appropriate to me as we strolled up to my "almost date." Rizzo pointed at her and told the kid, "Apologize to the lady."

"But I didn't . . . "

"Tell her you're sorry."

"I'm sorry, ma'am."

Rizzo released him and pushed him toward the front door. He turned to the woman who scowled up at him.

"Ma'am?" she said. He called me Ma'am?"

Rizzo smiled that perfect smile then sat on my barstool and struck up a conversation.

She pointed at the missing arm. "Nam?"

Rizzo nodded.

"Marine?" she asked.

Rizzo nodded again.

"Yeah, I thought so," she said. "Old bully boy out there never had a chance, did he?"

"Not really," he answered.

"My name's Nancy. I did two tours over there myself. Army nurse, 91st Evacuation hospital in Chu Lai"

"Rizzo, Charlie Rizzo."

***

They chatted for two hours there at that bar, neither of them drinking. She was like a jewel in a spotlight. She glowed when she was with Rizzo. Rizzo glowed himself, and the outcome was inevitable. They were married six months later. I had his back for that one; I was his best man. He will always be my best man.

# Adrift

## by T.A. Novak

It was a day to christen a new used boat bought by a friend of ours who kinda reminds me of the skipper of the USS Minnow. You do remember "Gilligan's Island," don't you? That skipper had a broad smile to match his broad belly. Well, that might describe three of the four men on our boat, maybe not the smile, but the belly part.

Unlike the people on Gilligan's boat, there were eight of us, not seven, all husbands and wives. For sure, there was no Ginger or a Mary Ann in the mix. We were all old, past our prime, and in need of ironing—if you get my drift.

Our voyage started out just fine, disembarking from Site Six with an hour cruise ahead of us toward a restaurant down by Havasu Springs for lunch. Somewhere down near the pipes that siphon the water to California, the ladies spotted three donkeys munching among the cliffs.

"Chris, slow down. There's some donkeys," one of the girls said.

"Oh, let's get a closer look," said another.

"They're so cute," another female voice cooed.

Chris, the captain, tried getting closer so someone could take pictures. He drifted a little too close, losing the direct line of sight to the donkeys.

"Back up," the captain's first mate, aka wife, said.

As Chris slowly started to back up, another voice shrieked, "Back up, back up, back up!"

Chris slammed the throttle to full speed to match Beulah's machine-gun-fire request. About one hundred gallons of Lake Havasu poured over the swim platform into the back of the craft, soaking two sitting ladies and the shoes of the other two standing.

"Hey, you're swamping us," yelled Beulah.

The boat had an automatic bilge pump, and the six inches of water on the deck of the back half of the twenty-three-foot Chris Craft pleasure boat quickly went away. Two wet butts and four sets of soaked shoes were the only casualties.

But Beulah had to bark at the captain. "You backed up too fast, got us wet, and now the donkeys are gone."

His second and third chin flapped as he echoed Beulah's orders. "You yelled, 'back up, back up, back up,' so I backed up." His smile had disappeared.

*That's all a man at the wheel of a strange boat needs is two back seat drivers and one that had to be Beulah. As usual, she had assumed command wherever she happens to be.*

Without saying it, I know a couple of the husbands were thinking that if you've seen one jackass, you've seen plenty, and now we had one sitting with us in the boat.

Lunch at the Springs went fine except two salads got mixed up and, low and behold, Beulah's had onions.

"I specifically said, NO ONIONS!" she carped at the waiter.

Another woman, who doesn't eat onions, quietly picked off her scallions because that's what they were. Scallions.

We took our time at the Springs, oohing and ahhing at the big carp, catfish, and one big striper that hung out around the boat docks.

We took off after a few minutes, heading north with the intent that Beulah's husband could throw a line in the water somewhere between Black Meadow Landing and the Standard Wash because that's where the morning paper had said the bait fish were hanging out.

Someone ordered the boat to be turned off so Dick could dip his line in the water. Guess who? Fifteen minutes later she checked her watch and barked another order. "Time to go. I've got a four o'clock phone call I have to take."

Only the boat wouldn't start. Oh, oh. The captain tried and tried—and tried. He tried so much he was depleting the battery. I'm not a mechanic, so when two of the guys said it sounded like the starter was bad, I had to agree.

There was one emergency paddle, and one of the guys and my wife took turns keeping us off of the rocks, moving us into the main channel, which was good. The wind and the current would take us toward Sandpoint and Cattail Cove, where we knew we could get some help.

Beulah's husband and I took a catnap on each side in the front of the boat while our new captain took over. It was 1:30 and she had a four o'clock phone appointment. She grabbed the white jacket she had been wearing, ran to the front of the boat, and started yelling and waving it.

"Help! Someone help!"

The nearest boat was one of those 250,000-dollar cigar boats that was going full blast and not giving a damn about a boat full of old people a half mile away.

The real captain's wife got on her cell phone, and through information got the number for Sand Point. It has a bar, restaurant, gas, and whatever, a logical place to call. The first mate talked to a woman who said she would try to find someone with a boat that would come out and tow us in.

In the meantime, Beulah kept yelling and waving her white jacket. Someone suggested she take her top off. That's when I finally had to say something.

"We want boats to come toward us, not run away."

I got a good scowl from Beulah for that remark.

In due time, a pontoon boat was leaving Sand Point. Beulah kept waving and yelling. The pontoon was heading north on an angle away from us.

"Don't them idiots see we've got an emergency?" It was Beulah talking.

Somewhere about a half mile away, the pontoon turned. They must have seen the white flag being waved. It was four ladies out for an afternoon cruise. They towed us in to Cattail Cove. The first mate had already called a friend to come down from Havasu so the captain could go get his truck and trailer and haul the broken boat in for repairs.

Problems arose because there was only room for three in the friend's vehicle. I thought I would go with our captain and get my truck and bring it back. I can haul five in it. Beulah demanded to go because she had this phone call to take and it was 2:45.

Edie reminded me that Beulah had first dibs on a ride so she could get to her car and go answer her phone.

I gave my wife my keys, saying, "I'll stay and help load the boat."

As we passed the time, waiting for the captain and my wife to return, I asked Beulah's husband, just out of curiosity, "Did you think we had an emergency?"

As always, he smiled and quietly said, "No."

He's got to love her, and for sure he's going to heaven. He's already spent too many years in hell.

## Stars and Beyond
### by Larry Quackenboss

    With DD-214 in hand, along with a lunch bag and my chemistry book, I walked—no, more of a march—into the employment office of North American Aviation.
    "May I help you?" the receptionist asked.
    My reply was, "I understand you are hiring, and I would like to fill out an application."
    She handed me an application, and I filled in all the blanks, signed it, and handed it back. I also gave her my DD-214 to copy and staple to the application form, which she did and handed it back to me, saying, "We're hiring only in select engineering positions, and as I glance over your app, I see you do not have a degree."
    Holding up my chemistry book I said, "I'm using my GI Bill to get a degree. What I need is a job to support my pregnant wife and a child when it comes. I've only been out of the Army six weeks and have spent that time enrolling in college and finding a place for my wife and me to live."
    "Well, I'll pass this on to the HR reps, and maybe they will have a match for your qualifications."
    "Not a problem," I said, walking over to the couch in the reception area. I opened my lunch bag, took out a sandwich, and began eating while reading my assignment.
    "We close at four PM, and you need to leave." The receptionist said.
    I closed my book and, with a smile, said, "I'll see you after classes tomorrow." She gave me the strangest look as I walked out the door. The next day I showed up, smiled, sat down in a chair, opened my lunch, and read a chapter for my history class.
    On the third day, she asked, "Don't you have someplace to go?"

"Nope, all my classes are from eight AM to one PM, and rather than study at the library, I thought I would come here and check on a job."

On the fourth day, I walked in, and the receptionist asked, "Can you work second shift?"

"You bet. In fact, it's perfect. I can increase my classes next semester."

"Okay, I have set up a pre-interview with the HR rep for the Data Processing Group. She'll call you back in a few minutes and go over all of the employment paperwork."

And that's how I became involved with the nation's space program, from the Apollo through the Delta rockets and beyond.

# Happy Birthday

By Daniel Fraga

Crew: Subcommanders: Cristal (Clearheart); Devon (Drog);

Troopers: Candyman; Suit; Rat; Trots; Jonsey; Hellyes; Chi; Sam.

The morning is dark. Not because of the weather, but from smoke and debris produced by ongoing fire-fights. Incoming ordinance continues overhead, but is intercepted by automatic defense systems.

Cristal calls out, "Devon, get everyone together, we need to fight our way through this place. Everyone check your gear and ammo and be ready to move in five."

"Move to where?" Devon asks.

"Well, we're going to take the Trelan outpost and kick their butts off this planet," Cristal replies. "We colonized it first, and damned if we give it up easy!"

"Candyman, Suit, Trots - you're with me. Jonsey, Hellyes, Chi - you're with Devon," Cristal instructs. "Rat and Sam will hold back for special ops onboard the Trelan ship. You guys know the play!"

"We won't let you down Clearheart!" Rat and Sam reply.

Just then a pulse gun blasts the wall behind them, showering them in powdered bricks.

"Holy crap," Trots semi-whispers, "that's far too close for comfort. Let's book!"

"I second that," Hellyes replies, coughing from the dust.

"Devon's group and mine will flank the Trelans, drawing them away from their ship. Rat and Sam will then work their magic." Cristal instructs.

"Affirmative sub-commander, all acknowledge as they move out."

*We really have a bit of a tactical disadvantage,* Devon thinks as they moved along the Trelan right flank. *With three sets of eyes and four 'arms' or whatever those things are, I would call that a tactical advantage. But, if we disable one for their three legs, they can't manage bipedal locomotion very well, and we can use that to our advantage.*

"Guys, did we all bring 'poppers' and slings?" Devon asks his crew.

"Of course, Drog," Jonsey replies, "and in case you don't remember, Hellyes and I are not GUYS!"

"Yeah, yeah, yeah," Devon replies, "don't go all literal on me dear. There's a lot to be said for 'generics', they make life simpler!"

On the left flank Cristal and her crew are in place. She radios Devon to confirm his team is ready as well.

"Okay Drog, on my mark let's surprise the heck out of these Trelans and draw them out." Cristal orders. On three, both teams release their first round of poppers.

Poppers are in essence small mines that can be deployed from a distance in numbers of ten to fifteen per shot. Within two minutes the Trelan command post is littered with a couple hundred of them, making it nearly impossible to move about.

"Good deployment," Cristal says through her comm, "now let's give them something to come after. Fire pulse guns at will and be ready with slings when they advance toward each team. We need to draw as many as possible away from their command post."

Even before her command is given, phase pulses are being directed at each team from the enemy. From their firing pattern it's clear the Trelan fighters only had a general idea where the teams are located, but trees and rocks surrounding the teams are rapidly being pulverized. Suit, Candyman and Trots receive grazing wounds, but no direct hits. Hellyes is hit full on and is out of the fight. Chi and Jonsey drag her to safety behind some rocks while Drog keeps up fire, drawing the Trelan fighters towards himself and away from where Hellyes is now hiding.

"Strategy seems to be working," Cristal relays through her comm. "Rat, Sam, you in place and ready?"

"Affirmative Clearheart, ready and raring," Rat replies. "just a few stragglers are left on base. Not sure if they are protecting it or just can't negotiate the poppers. Damn those things worked well, they took down about a dozen of them from what I can see."

Cristal asks Devon, "Drog…how many coming your way? We have eight or nine coming towards us, and a few still at their command post."

"There are twelve to fifteen coming our way. We'll deploy slings as soon as we get safely away from Hellyes," Devon replies.

"Roger that," replies Cristal. "Drog, you give the go ahead for sling deployment. Rat and Sam, be ready for your assault on the command ship on Drog's go."

"Roger that Clearheart, looking forward to it," Sam replies.

As Jonsey and Chi rejoin Devon, phase pulses are going off right and left, laying waste to their potential cover as they return fire. On the left flank Trelan fighters approach Cristal's team.

"Okay folks, time to boogy on these freaks," Devon instructs, "On three, deploy poppers and follow that up with slings. With any luck they'll be reduced to nothing but Trel-juice. Oh hell, I'm feeling impatient. THREE"

In an instant the Trelan fighters are showered in a new round of tightly thrown poppers. In addition they hear a strange humming as the slings head their way at high speed. Slings, perhaps the simplest of weapons, race towards the Trelan fighters and in less than a minute entangle their legs, arms, and any body parts the slings connect with. Each end of the sling has a small but potent popper that can take down a grown man. As Trelan fighters fall into the waiting poppers, they are indeed reduced to little more than puddles of former Trel.

Back at the alien base camp Rat and Sam have taken out the remaining fighters, discretely loaded the trans-phase device onto the Trelan ship, and retreated back to cover.

Clearheart and Drog's teams drive the remaining enemy back towards their ship.

As the Trelan ship takes off, the teams reunite and carry Hellyes back to base.

"Are we forgetting something?" Cristal asks, looking back at Sam and Rat.

"Oh yeah," Sam replies, and activates the trans-phase device.

In a blinding flash the Trelan ship is vaporized. The surrounding jungle flashes and disappears as the game ends.

"Wow" Cristal exclaims. "This was the best birthday present I've ever gotten! Thanks you guys." The team returns their gear to the prep station and say goodbye to the total immersion game room.

"We'll be back!" they all agree.

## High School Writing Contest

In 2017, the Lake Havasu City Writers' Group initiated a high-school writing contest not only to encourage literacy but also to expand interest and participation in creative writing. As an impetus to students' participation in the contest, cash prizes were awarded to the first, second, and third place entries. Those winning entries were published in the T*ales From Havasu* Vol 10 and the names of the winners were also highlighted on the back of the book jacket.

Because the LHCWG believes that all writers have had a mentor who encouraged them to write, the group is again providing aspiring authors a great opportunity to have a story published in a book that they can share with friends, family, and posterity. As in 2017, the LHCWG worked together with high-school teachers and administrators to encourage students' participation in the contest, and cash prizes have again been awarded to the authors of the three winning stories.

Enjoy reading the winning stories in the following pages of the *Tales From Havasu Vol 11*

# The Stain

## First Place Student Contest

by Kayla Maserang

I glared at the grimy, smoke-stained spot on the ceiling while lying on my warm foam bed. I felt nothing. I was an arrow without a target, no purpose or direction in life, just doomed to plunge to the ground, achieving nothing. Finally, with great effort, I dragged myself up and surveyed my room; clothes were scattered around my bed. Old cups and bowls cluttered the desk and the floor, and trash littered every flat surface. I had not cleaned my room in months, but even the notion of cleaning made me feel overwhelmed.

Exhausted from the endeavor of sitting up, I slumped back down on my bed.

*What is wrong with me? My room is a mess, and here I am lying back down? Enough!*

I lurched to my feet, staggering. I realized I had not eaten in days. What's the point anyways?

*So now what? I have gotten up. Am I going to clean now?*

I just couldn't muster any motivation, so I collapsed back onto the comfortable bed that seemed so detached from the world.

*I am a slob. Look at me. I look like a monster, and I am unable to even take care of myself. What would mom say, huh? She would be disappointed to have a pig for a daughter.*

Instantaneously, I jumped to my feet, this time tripping over a mountain of trash and clothes. Again, I tumbled, this time face-first onto the heap of my discarded life. My hand slipped into a moldy half-eaten ramen bowl that I had thrown aside a week before and had forgotten about. With my hand in the bowl, I lay there on the cold floor as if I were a corpse on a cold metal autopsy table, ready to be dissected and ripped apart.

*That is repulsive; get your hand out of there!*

I lifted my hand, attempting to shake the chunky remnants of the week-old ramen from my fingers and wiped the pungent-smelling broth on the stained clothes in front of me. On the cold, cold floor, I sat for countless hours, waiting for nothing.

*Get off the floor! It is filthy. I am lying next to a pile of trash.*

I dragged myself up and plopped onto the safety of my bed like a beached whale desperately trying to flop back into the sea. I grabbed my phone off the floor and became engrossed in a wormhole of asinine videos for countless hours. What's the point anyway?

*I've spent the whole day doing nothing. Am I just going to waste away my life like this? I'm so useless.*

I powered my phone down and stared at my tobacco-ridden ceiling as I had many times before. Each day, the blob of smoke stain grew larger and darker like a cloud before heavy rain. I prayed that the dark stain would grow big enough to engulf me and take me from my pointless life one day.

*So?*

So, what?

*This is why mom doesn't love me; I'm a horrible excuse for a person.*

I then rose, bent over, and picked up a loose candy wrapper. Warm tears started to well up in my eyes. My heart banged against my ribs, begging to escape my body. My lungs labored to breathe. Finally, I dropped the sticky wrapper back onto the litter-covered floor and lay back on the safe bed.

Crying for countless hours, I waited for nothing.

*Good-for-nothing.*

I pushed myself up, determined this time to clean my room. I lifted the loose candy wrapper, displacing the ants crawling on it. The crinkled piece of plastic somehow felt heavy in my hands. I crammed it into my pocket.

I then moved on to the putrid ramen bowl, draining out the sour contents. I lugged all the plates and bowls down the long hall to the kitchen, each item feeling lighter and lighter in my hands. I discarded the piles of refuse situated around my room and cleaned my clothes. Each mound I cleared revealed things I thought I had lost. I basked in the nostalgia of those long-forgotten items that I once held so dearly.

The only thing left to clear was the smoke stain looming above me. I hoisted myself up on the bed that brought me so much comfort. I sprayed vinegar and bleach on an old rag; the mixture overwhelmed my nostrils. I raised the rag to the ceiling, but something held me from finishing what I had started.

*Do it, idiot. Just wipe the smoke off.*

I couldn't.

And so, my room was **almost** spotless.

*I did a lot today, and I'm proud of the results.*

I plopped back on my bed with a faint smile creeping across my face. I felt satisfaction then happiness because I had finally felt something for once.

Just then, I heard the creak of the front door.

*It's probably just Mom. I hope she notices that I cleaned my room. She might be proud.*

Delicately, I opened the door and approached my mom, who was staring into the empty fridge.

"Hi, Mom."

"Hi, sweetie, how was your . . ." She turned around to face me. "You look horrible. Have you even showered? You look like you've gained weight too. You'll never find a good man if you keep looking like that," she stated with a condescending tone.

"No, I haven't showered yet, but did you see that I cleaned my room?" A lump started to form in my throat.

"Okay? Do you want a prize or something? I am not going to praise you for something you should be doing routinely." She scrutinized me up and down. "Geez, sweetie. We desperately need to get you on a diet . . ."

I sighed, "What's the point anyway?" The lump in my throat grew to fill my whole body, weighing me down with every step I took.

I plodded back to my room and stared at the spot on my ceiling. For countless more hours, I waited for the end.

# Seeds in the Wind

## Second Place Student Contest

by Laci Towner

Long ago, the world was not as it is today. Then, there were no forests, only one giant tree surrounded by endless nothingness. This big tree was called the Great Tree. The tree granted life to man and all the animals that lived beneath it.

One day, some seeds fell from the tree's tall branches, landing at the feet of The Chief. The Chief gently picked up the seeds, knowing that the tree was too important to leave them. Instead, he decided to take them to his pregnant wife to ask her what he should do with them.

"Well, we must care for such sacred seeds," said his wife after looking at them for some time. "The Great Tree is what gives us life; we should show our thanks by making sure they grow. However, I am not sure I can offer such care as I shall have our child very soon. You must care for the seeds on your own."

The Chief shook his head. "I cannot care for the seeds, for you are far more important. All my care goes to you and our soon-to-be-born child. I fear I will not have time for both tasks."

"This just won't do," said his wife, followed by a long pause. "Perhaps the animals can care for the seeds as they are granted life from the Great Tree as well."

A grin formed on The Chief's lips. "A splendid idea from a splendid woman!" he said. "I shall call the animals at once."

It was not long before all the animals were gathered beneath the tree, each curiously sniffing the seeds. The Chief explained that the seeds fell from the Great Tree and that they must be cared for.

The deer stepped forward. "I will care for the seeds. Put them on my head; they will be safe up there."

The Chief agreed and carefully set the seeds between the deer's velvet ears. As soon as the seeds settled, two small trees began to grow on the deer's forehead. Branches sprouted and leaves unfurled. The growth, much faster than any other plant growth, was clearly visible to the eye. All the animals watched in awe.

After a few minutes, the trees had grown more than twice the size of the deer's head, and he started to notice how heavy they had become. His tiny hooves began to sink into the ground, creating thin holes. Whenever the deer tried to lift them out, they would just sink into the ground again.

"I cannot care for these seeds," he said. "My hooves are too thin. They sink into the ground with all this extra weight."

The Chief quickly removed the seeds from the deer's head. As soon as they were gone, the leaves on the two trees turned brown and crumbled to the ground. All that was left were two dead branching stumps that are known now as handsome antlers. Without all the weight of the leaves, the deer was able to stand normally again.

"This won't do," said The Chief. "Someone else will have to care for the seeds."

This time the rabbit stepped forward. "I will care for the seeds; my feet are much wider. They'll be safe on my back."

The Chief agreed and carefully set the seeds on the rabbit's back. Once again, they began to grow, this time into thin blades of grass. The grass slowly covered the rabbit's entire body, leaving only her small nose and void black eyes exposed. She shook her body, admiring her new leafy coat. Suddenly, the grass began to droop, for the rabbit was not tall enough to reach the sunlight that the seeds needed. She quickly noticed this.

"I cannot care for the seeds, for I am too short to reach the sunlight."

The Chief sighed and removed the seeds from the rabbit's back. Without the seeds, the grass turned brown, becoming soft fur.

"This just won't do," The Chief said. "Someone else will have to care for the seeds."

This time the bird fluttered forward. "I will care for the seeds; I can fly up high where they will get plenty of sunlight. I can carry them safely with my feet."

The Chief agreed, and the bird took the seeds in his feet, flying up into the air. Long leaves began to grow from the seeds, trailing behind him beautifully in the wind. The bird flew higher and higher, up to where the wind was strong. He held on tightly to the seeds, but it was not enough; a strong gust of wind blew them out of his grasp. He tried to grab them, but the wind sent them far in every direction, spreading them all throughout the bare lands of the North, South, East, and West.

As the leaves on the bird began to die, becoming long tail feathers, the seeds sprouted all across the empty land. Flowers, trees, grass, bushes, ferns, and even mushrooms formed on the empty ground. The endless nothingness was filled with lush forests where man, animals, and all their children could live happily for generations.

# Morning Glory

## Third Place Student Contest

by Damari Campos

Elizabeth Annie Gold was her full name, but we called her Eli for short. She was not only my ray of sunshine but also my only child. As I sat back and watched her grow up on this planet Earth, I marveled at the strawberry blonde hair her grandma had given her, the freckles given to her by her papa, and the lovely green eyes that I had given her. I reminisce about the day she came into the world. The most perfect day started when my husband and I saw the two-line test and told the family and our friends. The grandparents thought, "Our first grandchild, a granddaughter" as a color of rose pink exploded from a balloon.

The doctor placed her on my chest, and my husband stroked her little golden locks. "Elizabeth," I thought and smiled as we drove home where she would grow up and become known as Eli and complete our family for the next few years. A wild adventure began as we were faced with diapers and sleepless nights. A mess became what we called clean, and crying sent us on a wild hunt.

Once while we were at the park and I held Eli in my lap while we sang, her father came around with strawberry ice cream. Eli hopped out of my lap and ran to her father; that was the first time she would ever walk. From then on, you could never stop Eli even if you were a track star. Eli ran and ran, but when she wasn't running around the house, she was with her dad. My husband and his little princess went everywhere together: to car shows, to the park, to the indoor playground. Often they would drive around the town.

When Eli felt sick, we all sat in to watch movies, and as Momma worried, Eli would smile and say it was just a cold. When Eli did cry, Momma hugged her and asked her if she wanted a band-aid for her booboo. One time when Eli was really sad and upset, Mommy and

Daddy explained that her tooth would grow back, but she could give the tooth to the tooth fairy. That next morning Eli woke up to a ten-dollar bill under her bed; the family went to get ice cream at the park that day as Eli smiled her new smile. The park was my little girl's favorite place, especially at Christmas when she unwrapped a bike. Every Christmas morning she would find thousands and thousands of toys from Mom and Dad. The park became her home as she spent time mastering a new challenge, the bike with no training wheels.

Soon, my little Elizabeth grew up, and the first day of school came rolling up, but unlike most kids, she gave me a quick goodbye kiss and ran towards her new adventure. School went by so fast that her first day of high school came and was followed by her first boyfriend. She didn't last long with him, but I still warned her: "Don't trust all the cute boys who offer you flowers." When she came home crying, I was there to comfort her, telling her how long it had taken me to find her father. We had girls' day out; we went shopping and bought her a whole new style, and I even let her dye her hair. By the time her dad came home, she held a driver's license, and her father was proud that, after all, his lessons had gotten passed down. That day, my daughter got her father's little red truck.

Eli progressed from elementary talent shows to middle-school track games and then to graduation. She finished high school with straight A's. I couldn't have been more proud. Eli and her friends smiled as I took pictures of the whole night while so many parents and I shared in their excitement. Aunt Linda gave her a hundred dollars, as promised, and her dad bought her the new car she had been eyeing. That night changed to the morning she went off to university and began to study engineering.

A few years passed, and Eli told me she had met the one. Before long, she showed me her engagement ring and then gave me a wedding invitation. The venue was set like a night in Paris, but all I really remember is she and her dad walking down the aisle. Elizabeth, my beautiful daughter, became Elizabeth Annie Lou. A few years later, I got a call, and before I knew it, I was a grandma to a sweet little set of twins. "Her growing up years happened so fast," I thought as I looked through family albums.

Today I'm driving past houses on my way to her home. I drive until I pass most neighborhoods; then, I take a sharp turn and park the car where there's a sign that reads "Cemetery." Holding flowers of all the pinks, I pass by where the older folk are buried and the grass is dead. I walk into a white-fenced area with lively grass and plant the flowers. I sit down, surrounded by morning glories, and my mind falls down to reality as the gravestone where the flowers are reads, "Elizabeth Annie Gold, May 18, 2022-May 18, 2022, Forever our Daughter."

The real memories flooded in and drove out the daydreams. The day Elizabeth Annie Gold was born a faint cry was heard before the doctors laid a silent baby on my chest. After that, I and my husband went home, and I cried and locked myself in her nursery. I was dealing with this new form of sorrow, and my husband tried to overcome his grief to understand mine. When it was time, we went among other grieving parents and purchased her slot in the graveyard, and I was distraught to know that such small coffins ever had to exist and that I had to purchase one. The funeral was small with mostly ultrasound pictures except for the one the nurses took where Elizabeth is dressed in a Minnie Mouse outfit.

Then we went to pay the hospital bill, and I had a bitter and cruel attitude toward the young parents who left with their family that was happy and perfect. "Why can't I have that?" I always asked. Today, I brought flowers not only to replace the dead ones from a few weeks ago but to show Elizabeth that I'd had another positive test. I should have been happy and filled with joy, racing to unpack the nursery, and running to tell my parents and husband. But I wasn't ready to go to the ultrasound or to be called "mother" by another child, and, to be honest, I didn't want it to be true. I wasn't ready to fill the album and be happy again because I didn't want to be the person who made a grieving parent bitter and jealous. All I thought was "Elizabeth Annie Gold was the most perfect child . . . would've been the most perfect child."

Made in the USA
Middletown, DE
19 November 2022